PECOS PUEBLO PEOPLE
THROUGH THE AGES
". . . and we're still here."

Stories of Time and Place

PECOS PUEBLO PEOPLE
THROUGH THE AGES
"... and we're still here."

Stories of Time and Place

Based on
Material by Ellen Alexander

Carol Paradise Decker

Illustrations by Ellen Alexander

SANTA FE

Sunstone books may be purchased for educational, business, or sales promotional use.
For information please write: Special Markets Department, Sunstone Press,
P.O. Box 2321, Santa Fe, New Mexico 87504-2321.

Book and Cover design ➥ Vicki Ahl
Body typeface ➥ Minion Pro
Printed on acid free paper

Library of Congress Cataloging-in-Publication Data

Decker, Carol Paradise, 1927-
  Pecos Pueblo people through the ages : "--and we're still here" : stories of time and place /
by Carol Paradise Decker.
     p. cm.
  ISBN 978-0-86534-823-3 (softcover : alk. paper)
  1. Pueblo Indians--Folklore. 2. Pecos River Valley (N.M. and Tex.)--Folklore. I. Title.
  E99.P9D34 2011
  398.20897'4--dc23

                    2011023344

WWW.SUNSTONEPRESS.COM
SUNSTONE PRESS / POST OFFICE BOX 2321 / SANTA FE, NM 87504-2321 /USA
(505) 988-4418 / ORDERS ONLY (800) 243-5644 / FAX (505) 988-1025

Dedicated to
The Pecos Pueblo People
Past—Present—Future

Special thanks for encouragement, connections and perspectives to
Mike King, Judy Reed, Mary Ellen Gonzales, Arnold Herrera,
and others.

Contents

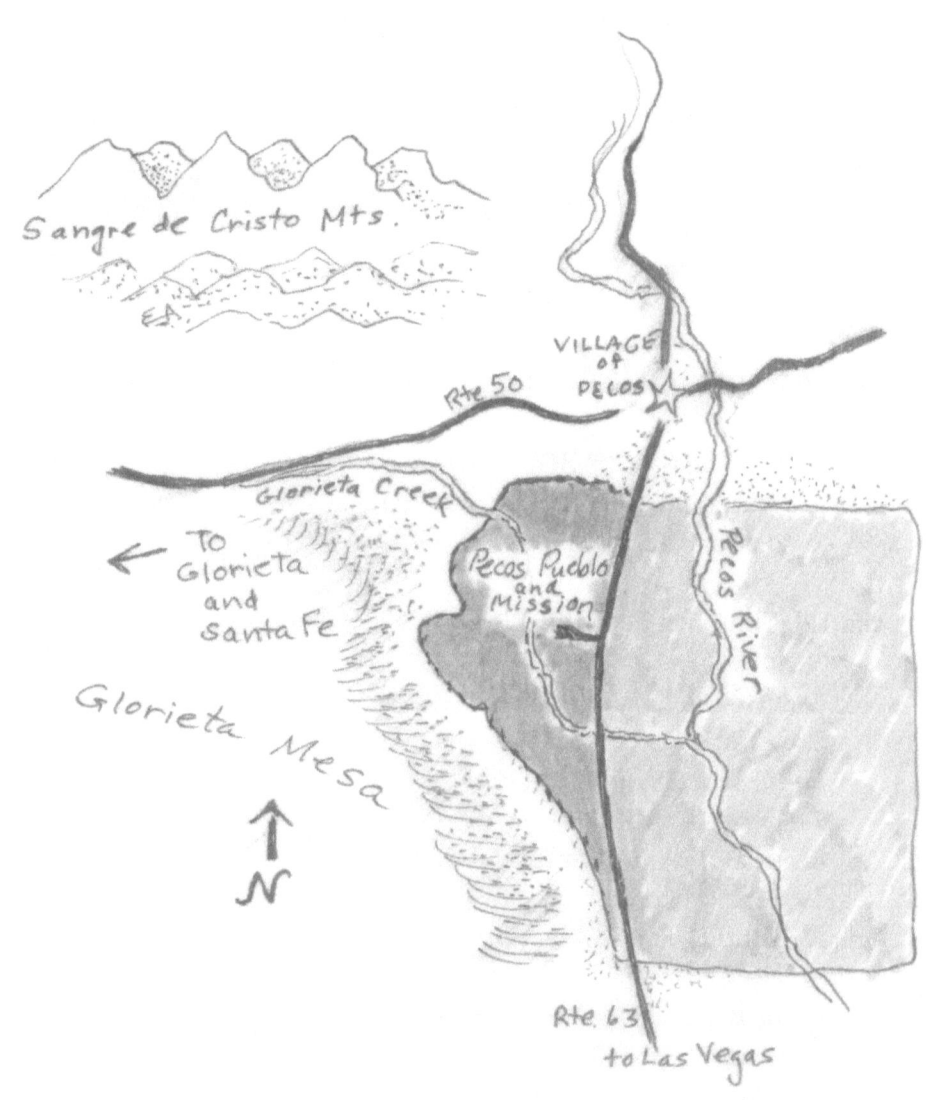

Pecos National Historical Park

Introduction

THERE'S A VERY SPECIAL PLACE in Northern New Mexico where the Pecos River emerges from the Sangre de Cristo Mountains into a beautiful, fertile valley. Clear and cool, the stream ripples over its shallow, rocky bed close to the eastern hills on its way to meet the Rio Grande far to the south in Texas.

To the west, the steep cliffs of Rowe Mesa tower over the valley. Horizontal bands of rock ledges interspersed with green vegetation glow rosy, orange, golden or tan in the changing light.

At the base of these cliffs, a small creek meanders along its way to join the Pecos River a little way downstream. Follow the cliff line to the south, and the ancient trail leads toward the Great Plains to the east. Follow it to the north toward the often snow capped mountains, and a gap to the west opens the way to Santa Fe and the pueblos along the Rio Grande.

People have passed through this valley for thousands of years. Some of them hunted the mammoths and giant bison, long extinct, leaving an occasional spear point to mark their passage. Others camped for a season, sometimes returning periodically to the fertile valley. Later, people settled permanently in pit houses, surface communities and the great Pecos Pueblo itself. Travelers, traders, armies, raiders and the great freight wagons of the Santa Fe Trail followed the rough roadway past the pueblo. And gradually, the small community of Pecos, surrounded by farms and ranches, took its present shape.

Much of the valley is now cared for as the Pecos National Historical Park. Its mission is "to preserve, protect and interpret" the resources of the area for all people. The core of the park is the narrow ridge on the western side of the valley where the humpy ruins of the pueblo and the red walls of the mission church dominate the view. The park also contains hundreds of other archaeological and historical sites, with more still being discovered.

As a park volunteer for five years, I guided hundreds of visitors along the Ruins Trail trying to help them visualize the life of the pueblo people and the influence of the mission church as they might have been. This book is my effort to expand on my stories of people who lived here over the centuries. Each focuses on the experiences of a young girl and some of her family members at times of change or crisis. A large bone bead, perhaps from a mammoth tusk, links the stories over the years.

The first three chapters visit with early inhabitants, temporary or permanent, separated by thousands of years. The middle five chapters feature moments in the life of the great pueblo at its height and in decline. The final two chapters focus on contemporary Pecos people and their relationship with their original homeland.

In many respects they are still here.

Part I

In the Beginning

Some twelve thousand years ago people were traveling through, and often stopping awhile, or permanently, in this lovely valley. The following three stories tell about some of them, separated from each other by thousands of years. Many changes had taken place in their lifeways, but the people themselves remained much the same.

1. Meat Today (8500 BC)

First came small bands of wandering hunters seeking the huge animals, now extinct, on which they lived. Life was hard and dangerous, but the People survived. Skilled at finding their prey, trapping and butchering and preserving the meat, they also used wild plants and smaller game. Much of what we know about them comes from the stone tools they left behind, the characteristic spear points, choppers, knives, awls and more.

2. Baskets and More Baskets (500 AD)

The people known loosely as "Basketmakers" found in the valley a rich source of the vegetable matter they used for shelter, clothing, sandals, snares, and particularly baskets of many sizes and shapes for different purposes. Some ancient baskets have been found in remote, dry caves in New Mexico, giving a glimpse of the weavers' skills. Some even had remains of the seeds and nuts stored in them. Pottery and bows were still in the future. Cultivation of small corn plants was just beginning, which required a new kind of relationship with the land.

3. Trade and Terror (1300 AD)

Much later, clusters of villages were spread out along the creek and the larger river. Houses, made of stone and adobe, were gathered around small plazas. The people farmed, traded, created pottery, wove cotton fabrics and were developing a rich ceremonial life. Most of the neighboring villages were friendly, but, occasionally, fierce strangers swept in to pillage and raid. This particular village, based on what is now known as the Forked Lightning Ruin, was beside the creek a short distance downstream from the later great Pecos Pueblo.

1

Meat Today (8500 BC)

WHAT WAS THAT SOUND? Small Girl jerked awake with a start. The gray light of dawn was seeping into the shallow cave where her family, a band of the People, was sleeping. The fire crackled and hissed and the light of new flames darted along the rock walls nearby.

Snap! There it was again. Small Girl giggled and snuggled back down in her sleeping robe. Her father was breaking sticks to build up the fire. When he saw her looking at him, he made chewing motions with his jaw and rubbed his stomach. She returned his grin.

Meat today! Yesterday, the scouts had found a small herd of bison, huge shaggy beasts with sharp horns. They were wandering up the valley following a small stream. If the scouts and older hunters were clever and lucky, they could urge the bison up the gentle slope of a nearby ridge and toward a cliff that dropped off steeply. If they kept just out of sight making small sounds and movements, they could make the nearsighted animals aware of their presence but not alarmed and moving toward the prepared trap.

Fresh meat roasting over the fire! Sizzling chunks of red meat filling mouths and stomachs! Blood and fat dripping down faces and arms. Strength returning to famished bodies! Small Girl smiled and her mouth watered in anticipation.

For too long the People had not found much meat, and they were hungry. Old One said the great herds were smaller and fewer each season, and it seemed he was right. Many moons they had searched in vain for the bison that sustained them. Sometimes the hunters brought home a deer or antelope, but generally those animals were too fast for the hunters' spears. Bears were dangerous and often hunters were killed instead of the beasts. Recently roots, wild onions, lizards or maybe a rabbit or two had been all they had found to eat. But today—MEAT!

Around her the huddled sleepers began to stir. Close by, Mother sat up and started to nurse the New One. This New One seemed strong and healthy. Perhaps he would live to grow up, as Mother's last two tiny ones had not. Other women, children, and the light-sleeping men stretched and yawned.

Pressed against the wall of the shelter, farthest from the light and warmth of the fire, the Old One slept alone. Small Girl felt an ache in her heart as her eyes outlined the small, dark form. Bent and brittle as an old tree, once famed as First Hunter, he no longer hunted with the other men.

The morning was cold. Small Girl pulled her shaggy sleeping robe around her shoulders as she reached for her sandal. Darkness came last night before she had finished repairing it. Now she stuffed some more dead grass between the two layers of thin bison hide that formed the sole and threaded the rawhide thongs through the holes she had punched with her bone awl. The sharp edge of the flint knife Old One had given her cut through the skins smoothly.

Old One was the best toolmaker of the People, and men of other bands traded eagerly for the things he made. He knew just where to strike a piece of stone to shape spear points, choppers, scrapers, knives. They were sharp and balanced and fit neatly to the shaft or to the hand. They were beautiful too.

But lately his hands had become swollen and clumsy, and all his joints pained him. Yesterday he had broken each of the three spear points he was fashioning. The three little boys had laughed at him, picking up the pieces and chasing each other with them. Old One had said nothing, but Small Girl could tell he was discouraged and angry at the boys' disrespect.

Old One seemed to be from a long time ago. On a thong around his neck he wore a carved disk of bone that shone in the sunshine or firelight. Small Girl had often heard the story of how it had been handed down to him by one who was long gone. He had received it from other ancient ones who had hunted the great shaggy mammoths, huge beasts with curving tusks, long flexible snouts and humps of tender fat meat between their shoulders. These animals had disappeared long ago, and Old One had never seen one.

She watched him as he crawled stiffly out of his sleeping robe and reached for his spear, ready to join the women and children for the last part of the hunt.

Small Girl's big brother, Square Toes, came running to the cave to report. He was one of the scouts, the not-yet-grown men who had been trailing the bison herd all night. The People gathered up their light skin tunics, their weapons and tools, and followed him out into the early daylight. Small Girl quickly tied on her repaired sandal and raced after them, though her head felt dizzy from hunger. Mother and the New One, along with a couple of the other women and the smallest children, would stay at the cave, tending the fire, building drying racks for the anticipated meat, and chasing away wolves and other hungry animals.

Small Girl had once seen Mother drive away a pack of wolves, rushing at them with a flaming branch, hitting their noses and scorching their fur until they slunk off. She wondered if she would ever be brave enough to do that. Father had told of meeting hunters from another band of the People who traveled with a pair of wolves accompanying them. They helped with the hunt and guarded the camp, and no, they didn't eat the babies. How strange that seemed.

The morning was cloudy with a strong wind blowing from the east. Perfect conditions for the hunt! Though the bison could not see well, they had an excellent sense of smell. The cliff was on the eastern side of the ridge. The hunters approaching from the west could stampede the bison toward the cliff where they would fall off and be killed or trapped in the boggy area below.

Square Toes led the people at an easy jogtrot, splashing through the shallow river and up to the top of the ridge. Small Girl had been here once before. She liked to look across the little pond to the rolling grasslands below and the mountains beyond. A small creek flowed between the west side of the ridge and the steep cliffs beyond. The bison were rambling up this valley and at the moment were out of sight.

In the dips in the surrounding land and along the riverbanks, bushes and stubby trees grew. These were scary places to Small Girl because wolves and long-toothed cats and snakes with rattling tails and poisonous bites lurked in the undergrowth, ready to pounce on the unwary. But the wood from such places was essential for fires, for tool handles, for spear shafts.

Hunters had used this place before, perhaps many times. Piles of rocks made rough walls stretching out from the steepest part of the cliff in a huge V. The wide end opened toward the gentle slope to the west, while at the cliff end, the V was so narrow that the huge animals could not turn around. It was an efficient trap.

Father and Old One directed the work as the people piled up fallen rocks and dragged dead branches to fill in the gaps in the walls. Everybody already knew what to do. Small Girl broke some green branches from a nearby pine tree and placed them beside the rock piles where people could grab them easily.

Square Toes, Father and most of the men went off to join the hunters following the herd. Older folks, women and children stayed to tend the trap. For the moment there was nothing much to do except to stay out of sight, be quiet, and wait.

⌒

Small Girl sat down beside Old One. His once springy stride had become a painful hobble and he seemed very tired, even though the sun, which had broken through the clouds, was not yet high. She wondered if this would be his last hunt and what he would do when he could no longer keep up with the People when they traveled from one campsite to another. Sometimes the People carried their old ones with them as long as they could, but Old One would never permit that. Sometimes an old one was left in a cave with sleeping robe, weapons and some food to fend for himself while the People moved on. Sometimes an old one simply walked away from the camp into the night to give himself to the lurking wolves. She wondered what Old One was thinking now. His hand was cupping the mammoth bone bead on his chest and he had a faraway look in his eyes.

Everything was quiet and peaceful as the waiting people lounged behind the piles of stones. The breeze blew through the grass, making swishing sounds. Some birds twittered down by the stream and a hawk whistled as it soared overhead. Crickets chirped in the grass. The air was cool, the clouds had blown away, and the sun was beating down on their bodies, making them sleepy. No sign of the hunters or the herd. They were still somewhere below the edge of the slope.

Old One grunted and pointed with his chin. A black shape was approaching, the first of the huge bison that followed. He was coming right toward the middle of the wide end of the V. The hunters were doing their work well.

Alerted, the people crouched tensely behind the piles of rocks, keeping low, still, out of sight. The beasts ambled on, nibbling at tufts of grass, unaware that the stone walls were pushing them closer together, deeper into the trap.

Small Girl felt scared. The animals were so big, their long horns so sharp. What if she sneezed and frightened them away? She was so tense with excitement that she trembled all over. She clutched her pine branch—and waited.

"HAI-EEE!" First Hunter screamed the signal and those following leaped up, shouting, brandishing their spears, rushing toward the herd. The confused animals huddled together in a startled mass, not knowing where to turn. When the roaring group of hunters reached them and the first spears found their mark, the bison panicked. The whole herd broke into a run. But each time they tried to turn to the left or to the right, two-legged creatures jumped up from behind the rock piles, yelling and waving arms, branches, spears, pieces of hide, frightening them back toward the middle.

Small Girl waited for the herd to reach her. She felt the earth trembling as they came closer, closer. Now they were here, running right at her. Frozen with fear, she stared at their sharp horns, their foaming mouths, their red eyes rolling wildly in the huge black heads.

One of the beasts, trying to escape, ran right at her. Surely it would trample her. But Old One beside her screamed, "AY-AY-YA-YA-YA!" and whacked its nose with the side of his spear. The animal swerved back toward the others. Its hip and flailing tail as it turned knocked Small Girl down, but she leaped up quickly, hollering and waving her branch, somehow no longer afraid.

The first bison reached the point of the V, saw the precipice ahead and tried to stop or turn around. But the rocky walls had closed in, the howling two-legged creatures were close, the rest of the stampeding herd shoved from behind, and over it went. Then the others went bouncing off the rocky ledges onto the rocky ground below.

The last of the bison disappeared. The dust cleared. Small Girl and the others peered over the edge of the cliff. Some of the animals had survived the fall and were running off. Seven of them lay heaped or sprawled on the ground. Some of the hunters were already among them, their spears quickly finishing off those that were still kicking.

⌣

The people carefully clambered down the cliff, shouting with joy at the successful hunt. MEAT today and for a long time to come. But this was not the time to celebrate. There was too much work to be done. It took eight grown men to turn over the first carcass and move it to a flat place where it could be butchered.

First the ceremony. Old One was given the honor of the first cut. His sharp flint blade cut through the thick hair and hide to open the throat, and women caught the still flowing blood in gourds. Old One poured some on the ground in thanks, and the gourds were passed around among the people, each of whom took a mouthful of the hot blood. Next, Old One's blade opened the belly of the beast and sliced off a large piece of the steaming, still pulsating liver. He held it high in respect for the spirit of the bison. This too was passed around, each person biting off a piece. The blood ran down their chins, and they felt the warmth and strength of the bison sustaining their lives and strengthening their bodies for the work ahead.

The butchering went quickly, for the people were well practiced. Everyone had a job to do. They had to work rapidly before the bodies cooled and stiffened. Flint knives flashed and slashed. Strong hands peeled off huge pieces of hide. Sharp tools cut out big chunks of meat: tongues, livers, humps, great hunks from shoulders, legs, rumps, ribs. Hammer stones smashed bones and skulls for the tasty marrow and soft brains inside. Choppers broke apart joints so that bones could be separated and brought to camp. Bone awls picked out the long, tough sinews to be used for sewing and tying things together. Women carefully removed the huge stomachs to use as water bags and for storage, and sections of intestines, which when dried and tied at the ends made containers for needles and small tools. Men selected certain of the bones to fashion into spear points, digging sticks, clubs and ornaments. Old ones gathered some of the hoofs and horns to use in ceremonies.

The pieces of hide were heavy. The shaggy hair on the outsides was matted with mud and sticks and bugs, while the insides were coated with layers of fat and gristle. Small Girl knew that later she would help the women scrape and scrape and scrape and clean the hides until they were smooth and soft and could be used for sleeping robes, shelters, carry bags, moccasins. But for now, they were wrapped around piles of meat and bones for transportation back to camp. Many trips were necessary with watchful hunters accompanying each group, their spears ready and their eyes alert. Fresh meat and the smell of blood attracted wolves and other predators that would attack a lone or careless carrier.

Later, Small Girl would help her mother and the other women cut the meat into thin slices to dry in the wind and sun until they were hard and light, would be easy to carry, and would not spoil for a long time. Her father and Square Toes and the other men would shape the bones into useful objects. Younger children would clean and separate the long sinews and pack them in intestine tubes. The little ones would chase the flies and birds and foxes away from the drying meat. And everybody would eat and eat and eat.

At one point when Small Girl (she wasn't so "small" any more, she was almost as big as Mother and could work all day like a grown-up) stood to stretch her back, she spied Square Toes and another scout carrying someone between them. It was Turtle, battered and bloody, with one leg dangling uselessly. She heard Turtle's mother's howl of distress echoed by other women. A crippled son was a tragedy for the whole band. Some of the stampeding bison had broken away from the others, and when Turtle tried to turn them back they trampled him badly.

Old One, a respected healer, examined the boy where his friends had laid him. Bruises and cuts were not serious, but the leg? Broken. Small Girl watched as he wrapped a piece of hide around it and followed the boys as they carried Turtle back to the cave. She knew Old One would wet a piece of rawhide and wrap the leg with bundles of special herbs plastered around the break. As the rawhide dried, it would shrink and harden, making a stiff, supportive shell around the leg. With luck the leg would heal, maybe straight, maybe crooked. Or, in spite of Old One's skill, it might get infected and then Turtle would die. They would have to wait and see. Small Girl felt particularly sad because Turtle had always been kind to her, and in her dreams she hoped some day he would be her mate. But there was work to be done, and she returned to her task of picking long sinews from a backbone.

⌐

When Small Girl finally returned to the camp, staggering under a bundle almost as big as she was, meat was roasting on the fire. It smelled wonderful, sizzling and dripping fat. There were tender hunks of hump, rib bones thick with rich and tender meat, pieces of tongue suspended on green sticks and so much more. Darkness had come, and another fire blazed outside the cave where the scouts were to guard the bundles of meat throughout the night. Turtle was sitting there among the others, his leg stretched out in front of him while the rawhide casing dried. He was gnawing a fat piece of meat Square Toes had brought him. Juicy fat was dripping down his chin. Small Girl was glad to see him, especially when he grinned at her.

Small Girl picked up the two fine leather bags she had made several days ago. She was proud of the tight seams and the way she had greased the leather so that the bags would hold water. She filled them down by the river's edge, peering carefully all around in the darkness. They were too heavy for her to carry, so she quickly tied thongs around the openings and dragged them back to the fire where the drinking gourds were piled.

Everybody was eating the hot, sizzling meat, grunting with pleasure. Small Girl pulled a piece of rib bone out of the fire. It burned her fingers, but the meat on it was fat, rich and tasty. Oh so good!

She looked around for Old One. He was huddled in his sleeping robe, too tired to move. She pulled another section of rib from the fire and brought it to him along with a gourd full of water. As he sat up to bite off the meat with his few remaining teeth, the firelight reflected on his brown, wrinkled face. The carved bone bead gleamed white against his chest. She knew he believed it brought him blessings from the ancient spirits.

Old One put down the cleaned-off bone with a sigh of thanks. His eyes studied the girl over the rim of the water gourd for a long time. "You are no longer Small Girl," he said at last. "You are Almost a Woman. That's a better name for you now." He lifted the thong over his head and placed it around her neck. The bone bead felt heavy and warm against her skin. He pulled his sleeping robe around him again and lay down to rest with his back to her.

〜

Who was she now? Small Girl or Almost a Woman? She felt pleased and confused. And this precious bone bead? What did Old One mean by giving it to her? Was it to bring her wisdom and power from the Ancient Ones so she could help and care for the People as Old One had done? Was that too much responsibility for a young girl to carry?

Stomachs were full, drinking gourds were being passed around, as the exhausted people lingered around the fire. By its flickering light, some of them worked, the men examining and repairing their tools, women mending clothing or nursing their babies, children nodding off to sleep.

Mother was working on a rabbit skin robe for New One who was sucking happily on a piece of fat.

And now people began to talk, retelling in words and gestures the exciting events of the day, remembering details of other hunts, recalling places where they had roamed or camped, speaking of past hunters and skilled women and respected old ones.

Small Girl, now Almost a Woman, snuggled in her sleeping robe beside Mother, listening drowsily to the talk. She noticed that Old One had joined the group around the fire. For a while he just listened and nodded his head as some of the men pranced around, acting out hunting scenes with much laughter and teasing. Then Old One began to add his own stories. People listened with interest and respect, even though they had heard most of the stories many times before. He told about the huge camels and giant ground sloths and the long-ago mammoths that the Ancient Ones had hunted and old ones had described, though no one now had ever seen them. He described encounters with wolves and cave bears and long-toothed cats, and about outrunning antelope in his youth. He talked about other bands of the People he had met, and how sometimes they traded tools and supplies and information and sometimes fought and killed each other. He gestured toward One Ear and Quiet Woman who had been brought from other bands to join the family, both of whom worked hard, cared for their new men and children, yet often seemed sad.

As Small girl, now Almost a Woman, listened to Old One's voice, she saw the full moon rise above the cliffs across the stream. Right now, in this place, life was so good! She wished she could stay here, in this beautiful valley, forever.

But by the time the round moon came again, their work here would be finished. The People would pack up all they had—their robes, tools, dried meat—in their leather carry-bags. Mothers would settle their babies and small children on their hips. Backs would bend under the weight of their burdens. Spear-carrying hunters would guard the procession. And they would go off again. Would Old One and Turtle be among them?

Where would they go? Only the hunters and old ones seemed to know. As long as she could remember, they had roamed in search of the bison herds, often returning to familiar camps, sometimes wandering into new territory. Along the way, they lived on small game, wild plants, and what was left of the dried meat. When a herd appeared, the hunt would begin again—the killing, the butchering, the drying of the meat, the preparation of the hides. The never-ending work of gathering plants, food and firewood, of toolmaking, of working the heavy skins into clothes and shelter, the constant cycles of people being born, dying, growing, working, producing new ones. The wisdom of the old ones who appealed to the spirits, thanked the creatures that gave them life, healed the sick and injured and kept the memories of the People.

Would life ever change? When and where had it started? Where were they going, and why? As for her, would she grow up brave and strong like Mother? Would she have a man like Father—or like Turtle? Would she grow up to have her own children that would follow the herds as they did? Would she have the knowledge and power of Old One to share with the people in her band? Would she come back to this same spot and watch the same moon pouring its beautiful white light on this same stream?

She curled her fingers around the bone bead and felt its weight and its warmth. She knew it would help her for whatever lay ahead. She would have to listen carefully to Old One and the other old ones, both men and women in her band, and learn everything she could about—everything!

But now she felt cozy and comfortable. As she drifted off to sleep, she thought of the work to be done tomorrow, of the bison meat in her stomach, of food for the People, of the warmth of the cave and of the family of which she was a part. She was content.

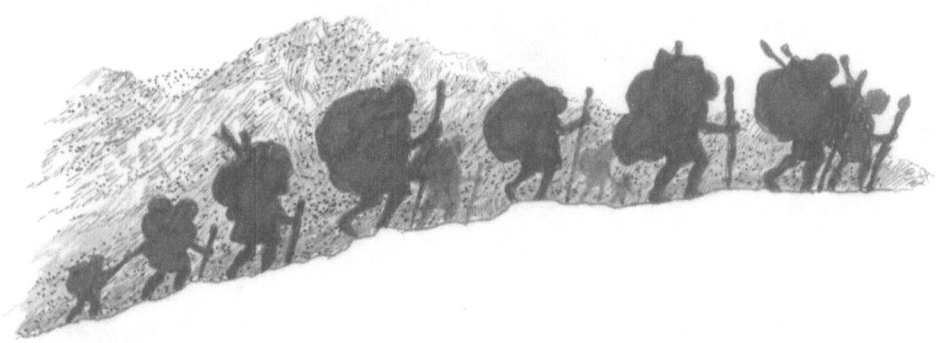

2

Baskets and More Baskets (500 AD)

GIRL WHO WONDERS was in a blue funk. Of course she wondered about everything, and of course she asked questions. Generally there were no answers. Today, even her mother had scolded her, telling her to shut up and look around at things as they are. And stop asking so many questions. And her friends had started teasing her, asking her ridiculous questions and laughing at equally ridiculous answers. They called her "Wonders," though she really wanted to know.

And then there were the baskets. Baskets, baskets and more baskets. Weren't there enough already? Piles of them under the shelter. Big conical ones with sturdy carry-straps. Strong, waterproof ones for cooking. Tightly woven ones for storage, many with covers. Flat ones for sorting things. Small ones for seeds. And everything in between, of all sorts and shapes and sizes, for all sorts of uses.

The one she was working on was almost finished. She jabbed her bone awl through the coils around the rim and yanked the thin willow strip through the gap that would complete the basket. Her baskets were never good enough, she lamented. They always leaked or gapped where they shouldn't or developed holes or were the first ones the mice destroyed. Even the mats she wove of flattened rushes unraveled around the edges, while her soft carry-straps and belts were too stiff to be comfortable. Even the yucca fiber sandals she made, though they looked beautiful, fell apart quickly. Now this basket. Would it hold water? She doubted it. She felt frustrated and fed up.

The fall sunshine warmed her back. Her small mat was just outside the brush shelter where some of the women were working. She heard the chattering of their voices and the scrunch, scrunch, scrunch sound of the hand stones on the surfaces of the hard stone slabs, as they ground seeds and acorns into coarse meal or powdery flour. Sometimes, one of them would start to sing and the others would join in their grinding, catching the rhythm. A couple of children were cleanings sticks and burrs from a basket of rice grass seeds. Grandfather sat nearby, carving an animal figure on a bone pipe with a sharp piece of flint. All seemed peaceful at the summer camp. But Wonder did not feel peaceful.

As long as she could remember, her family had spent the warm season with their band of the People in this valley. It was a fine place, and sometimes they had to fight with other bands that wanted to share it. A stream ran through it; fish, turtles, frogs and beavers lived in it. Other creatures came here to drink. Flat areas nearby were damp and soft, good places to tend the small corn plants the people had begun to cultivate. And everywhere, there were plentiful reeds, grasses, green shoots, flexible roots, fibers from the sharp-tipped cactus leaves, all sorts of plants useful for weaving the objects that made their lives so comfortable. From the time she could barely walk, she helped her mother gather materials and learned the weaving skills she would need.

Learned? Yeah. Baskets that leaked. She could cover the outsides with pitch, which she had done before, but that wasn't the point.

She studied the one she had just finished, tuning it round and round in her hands. It looked strong and sturdy with the fibers snugged tightly together. Would it work? Maybe? Her father and older brother teased her that she would "never be a woman" until her baskets could hold water.

She wondered why such baskets were so important when there were so many other things to be done before she "became a woman." She wondered how her people had learned to weave so many useful things and who had first found this valley so rich in seeds and plants and foods that they could preserve for the cold months ahead. She wondered who had first thought of planting and tending the little ears of corn in the damp soil a little way upstream, and where the corn seeds had come from in the first place. She wondered how her people in this band would be able to carry all they had gathered to their cold-weather camp. She wondered what Grandfather had seen during his long life and how true were the stories he told beside the evening campfires. She wondered what it would be like to have a man like Father and children of her own. She wondered—so many things. Everybody probably wondered, but she was the only one who asked questions. No wonder they called her "Wonders." And today she resented it.

~

"Come on, Wonders! Let's go!" Her cousin's voice broke into her thoughts. The piñon nuts were ripe now, and many women were gathering them. They provided nourishing food for the cold season. The other girl was getting impatient.

Grabbing a different basket, one with a head strap, Wonders followed the older girl. "It's late," complained the other. "It will be dark soon. If we can't gather enough piñons today, the mice and the birds will have eaten them all up by tomorrow, and we'll starve when the cold weather comes."

"Why do you worry so much?" asked Wonders, catching her breath as they clambered up the mesa toward the clumps of piñon trees. "There will be plenty to eat. We'll have amaranth and sunflower seeds, prickly pear, dried meat and fish and roots to bake in the coals. And acorn paste for thick stews and lots of dried grasshoppers. It looks as if our corn harvest will be plentiful, and our hunters will bring in deer and rabbits and maybe a bear or two. Don't worry, we'll have plenty to keep you fat."

Her cousin grinned and tugged at her hair. Wonders realized that she had been joking all along, and she felt foolish. It did not help her mood.

They paused on a ledge and looked back at the valley below. The shelter they had just left was surrounded by a cluster of small summer huts made of brush and matting tied down securely with long fiber cords. Smoke drifted up from cooking fires, and they could hear the distant scrunching of the grinding stones and the singing of the women. It was a comforting scene of peace and plenty.

As they clambered farther up the slope, they met some of the women coming down, their baskets laden with the small nuts. A couple of children carried rolls of matting that they had spread out under the trees to catch the nuts falling out of the cones when the women shook the branches. Wonders, reminded, wished she had remembered to bring a mat. Trying to find the little nuts when they had fallen into the grass and weeds was slow and difficult.

"Hello, Daughter! Did you finish your basket?" Wonder's mother was approaching with the others. "Don't stay too long up there. There are bears about, and you're not much use to us inside a bear's stomach. We need you back at camp." Mother's eyes smiled at the girls as she passed. She leaned her head into the carry-strap of the basket on her back and shifted Baby Brother astride her hip as she watched the trail ahead very carefully.

Wonders growled under her breath and considered what it might be like in a bear's stomach. The way she had been feeling today she might as well be there.

⌒

The nearby trees on top of the mesa had been well picked over. There were few nuts left. Her cousin wandered off toward the sound of voices Wonders recognized as girls from the camp. But she wanted to be alone. On a high limestone outcrop, she noticed a large stand of piñon trees. No one seemed to be up there. She pulled herself up, her feet and fingers wedged in cracks in the rock. Her hands grabbed the roots of a juniper tree. Soon, she was picking lots of the small nuts from some of the lower cones and from where they had fallen on the ground.

A rustling in the brush nearby startled her. Was it a bear? She realized that the sun was getting low in the sky and the shadows long and spooky. She panicked. She didn't really want to be eaten by a bear. She turned back the way she had come and began to run.

WHAM! Suddenly she was on her stomach, halfway dangling over the cliff. Her right leg was caught on something. Her basket had tumbled onto the slope below, scattering the nuts in the grass.

Wonders reached around for something to help her up. Her elbow hurt, her knee was skinned, and there was nothing, no root nor branch, no projection of rock she could grab for support. If whatever was holding her foot should break, she would tumble head first onto the rocks. Nobody responded to her call for help. She felt alone and scared. It was getting cold, and she wished she had her rabbit-fur cloak. Her thick grass skirt was not very warm and she wore nothing above. What if her mother had been right about bears? She knew they gathered when the nuts were ripe, and what would happen if one of them found her before one of her people did? She was stuck. She struggled against the tears welling up.

"Well! Look what I've caught here!" The voice was familiar and amused. Her brother, Rabbit Ears! Her relief at being found gave way to giggles. Poor Rabbit Ears! What bad luck he had in hunting. His nets always broke and the prey escaped. His snares got trampled or destroyed or the wolves reached his captives before he did. His perfectly straight spears when flung from his atlatl, his throwing stick, missed their target. And now he had caught HER!

Her giggles turned to laughter, as much in sympathy as in ridicule.

"Hey there, Big Hunter! At last you caught something worthwhile. ME! Just don't try to eat me. What were you planning to catch with such a strong snare? A bear?"

Rabbit Ears pulled her back up on the ledge and released her foot, but he said nothing. His jaw twitched in a way that Wonders knew hid his frustration. No matter that he tended the corn in the patch beside the river so carefully that it grew faster and bigger than anyone else's. No matter that he could reach into the water so gently that he could tickle the tummy of a fish and flip it out on the bank. No matter that the yucca sandals he made never fell apart. No matter that he could make flutes out of birds' wing bones and play melodies that haunted and delighted, particularly the women as they worked at the grinding. No matter that he had the patience to bore holes in bits of shell and bone and stone to make necklaces and ornaments that people were pleased to wear. No matter that he could chip bits of stone into spear points or knives more skillfully than anyone else in the band. None of these things mattered if he did not bring in the meat and skins that were the signs of a real man.

They clambered carefully down the cliff. While Wonders picked up her basket and tried to find as many of the spilled piñon nuts as she could, Rabbit Ears sat on a nearby rock and watched and waited. He was Almost a Man now, and gathering nuts and seeds was the work of women and children. And since Wonders was soon to be a woman, she should never touch his weapons or hunting gear

Wonders sensed his movement and looked up. Rabbit Ears was standing poised with a short spear set in his the notch of his atlatl. The throwing stick increased the length of his arm, propelling the missile with great force. But a low branch deflected the spear and it fell clattering on the rocks. Wonders saw the back of a deer scampering off among the trees.

Rabbit Ears slumped down on his rock, holding his head in his hands. Finally, he looked at Wonders and confessed, "I was too eager. I forgot the prayers to the spirit of the animal." He got up and went off to retrieve his spear.

Soon he returned. "Come on," he insisted. "It's getting dark and we need to return to camp."

Wonders, still trying to gather the spilled nuts, reluctantly followed him down the trail.

As they neared the camp, a voice hailed them. "Ho, Mighty Hunter, what are you bringing in today?" It was their father, approaching the camp from another direction, carrying a deer draped over his shoulders.

"Today I captured THIS!" responded Rabbit Ears as he made a grab for Wonders who ducked away laughing. There was a special note of fierceness in her brother's voice as his father teased him. They walked along together, and Wonders, following, heard Father saying, "That spear point you made for me yesterday is sharp and well balanced. You did a good job with it and it brought down this deer."

⌒

Back at camp, Mother was standing, stretching her back after a spell at the grinding stones. "Tend to the stew, then get some water, and take Baby Brother with you," she requested.

Wonders went over to the cooking fire. A watertight basket was half buried in the ground beside it. The water was steaming, aromatic with herbs and roots and wild onions. Stones, red hot from the coals, heated the stew efficiently. She picked up the pinchers made of a doubled-over green branch tied with a bit of rawhide and fished out of the stew a couple of cooled stones and replaced them with hot stones from the fire. She had dreaded this task ever since she dropped one of the stones on her foot. The angry red scar from the burn still pained her. She added a bit of rabbit meat from a nearby basket and a scoopful of acorn flour, stirred it a bit with a carved bone, and watched as the water began to bubble again.

Empty baskets were heaped beside the brush shelter. Others, filled with various foodstuffs, along with some leather bags and large gourds, were covered with mats just under the roof. During the day, small children watched over these baskets to keep the mice and squirrels away, while two of the old women guarded them at night. A couple of foraging rats could quickly destroy days of work and provisions for the people for weeks.

Wonders picked up one of the watertight baskets, set her little brother astride her hip, and headed for the river. At her favorite spot, a rock protruded out into the stream where the water ran deep enough to fill her basket easily, while along the shore the water rippled shallowly over a muddy bank.

She lingered a bit while filling her basket. The moon had just risen, making the river and surrounding landscape glow with white light. She enjoyed the beauty of it all, and the momentary solitude. She watched the baby playing in the mud. He had scooped up a large lump of soft clay and was patting it into a round ball. Then, gathering all his baby strength, he punched his little fist into the clay and giggled. He placed it carefully on a rock and scrambled off, protesting when Wonders picked him up to return to camp.

⌒

The people were coming into camp from field and forest, tired and hungry. Some lugged digging sticks or stone or bone blades attached to wooden handles they had been using in the corn patches. Others had been hunting and carried their spears and atlatls or fine-woven nets, along with the rabbits, small animals, fat birds and fish they had captured. Some women brought baskets of seeds or piñon nuts, and two girls had found some late-season blackberries. The cook fires were welcoming, the air was rich with aromas, hunks of deer were roasting in the stone-lined fire pit, and the small children were settling down to sleep. Wearily, the people sank down by their family fires, scooping the prepared food from the cooking baskets with gourd ladles, slurping and pulling out choice bits with their fingers.

Later, the people gathered around the central fire outside the main shelter. They shared stories of the events of the day, the things they had observed, the state of the wild crops and the corn. Wonders wondered if Rabbit Ears would tell about capturing her in his snare or about missing the deer, but to her relief he did not. Too much teasing would result.

The farmers reported that the green corn in many fields was ready to harvest; but if they let it dry on the stalks, it would be easier to handle, if the bears that had been seen in the area didn't get to it first. The nights were getting colder, and they began to talk about moving south to their winter campsite and all the things they needed to prepare for the journey. When they had come north in the spring, they had little to carry and were able to travel together in one group. But now, with their many bags and baskets of foods and hides that would see them through the winter, they would need to make several trips.

Wonders heard Father's voice among the others. Everybody respected his knowledge and judgment, and they listened to him as they made their plans. One group of the band would carry all they could to the winter campsite where they would repair the shelters, clean out the stone lined fire pit, welcome other bands of the People who would join them there, and protect their site from intruders. Others would stay in the valley to finish harvesting and would follow later. Some of the sturdy men and women would travel back and forth several times, helping lug the baskets, bags, mats, skins, tools, weapons, and all the necessary items. Strong men with sharp spears would stay with each group to repel the human raiders who sometimes robbed the people of their hard-won supplies or the four-legged bears and huge wolves that threatened

Wonders, her mother, baby brother and Grandfather would go along with the first group. Though she liked the summer camp in the valley, she liked the winter camp too. The journey took several days of walking downstream along the river to a place where overhanging cliffs protected the stone and brush shelters beneath them. The shelters were sturdy and warm while cold winds and storms of snow swirled around them. Large supplies of food would be cached in pits and crevasses where they would be available all during the cold weather. New layers of clay would be added to the old stone fire pit where whatever meat the hunters brought in would be roasted for all to share. Big piles of firewood would be collected, and many of the skins and hides they had prepared during the summer would be fashioned into tunics, leggings and robes to keep them warm.

Some of the other families coming to join them they had known for years. Others would be newcomers, for the overhanging cliffs stretched out along the river for a long way. While they sat around the fires repairing tools and making new ones, carving pipes and mending moccasins, they would share stories of their experiences over the past months and retell some of the ancient tales from long ago. Romance was always in the air as young people from different bands came together. Wonders was eager to reconnect with old friends, especially one of the young men she especially liked from the last season. When the first new green plants began to sprout, they would all pack up and leave for their summer camps, and the cycle of planting, tending and harvesting the corn, of gathering wild foods, and of making the all-essential baskets would begin again. Wonders was ready to go. She needed a change of scene and of people and some new challenge to her attention. But no more baskets, please.

⤸

From the other side of the fire, Wonders heard men's voices mumbling. Grandfather and the other older men were complaining among themselves. They were much respected by the people for their experience and their wisdom, but they belonged to an older time. The men of Father's age were now the acknowledged leaders.

Father's voice rang out, "Old Ones, what are you saying? Let us hear your words."

Grandfather spoke for the others, "We miss the old days. It is not good, this business with the harvests. It is a waste of time. We can no longer follow the herds because we must stay here in one place and tend those silly little plants." His voice rose with emotion. "The bison and the antelope and the mountain sheep wander freely while the men sit here in the cornfields."

Another of the men agreed, "Even the deer are laughing at us. We tend the corn all day and at night the deer come and eat it. We should be eating THEM!"

"What has happened to our great hunters?" added a third man. "Now our brave hunters are satisfied with the little animals, the small deer and the rabbits. It takes no skill or courage to take them down. And they hunt only when the corn and the piñons allow them to."

"It's true," moaned Grandfather. "We let the plants run our lives."

"Grandfathers!" It was Mother's voice. She was one of the few women who dared to speak what was on her mind. She was waving a bone from the deer Father had brought in, and the little bit of roasted meat still attached smelled delicious. "You think the hunt is everything, as it was in your youth. It is true that in the old days we depended on the herds, and great hunters like you kept us alive by your skill. But life was so hard! Always we had to keep moving, dragging our old people and babies and all our possessions with us. The bison wandered far and wide, and without them we had nothing. People died before their time. They were killed by the animals they hunted, or they starved when none could be found. Or sometimes they just died from the struggle to keep up with the band, carrying heavy loads through rain and snow day after day. Thus my grandmother died and her first-born was eaten by one of the wolves that always followed the hunt."

"But then the great herds would appear." Grandfather was almost shouting. "And we feasted on bison meat until we almost burst. How many of us here can remember the rich taste of that meat? And the winter-warmth of a thick bison-hide robe. Now our women spend too much time sewing together tiny strips of rabbit fur for blankets. The old ways were better. This tending of tiny plants that don't even come up half the time will not last long. And then our young men will return to the hunt. And we shall eat and grow fat!"

Father's calm voice broke into this outburst, "Grandfathers, the people would not be here if it were not for your knowledge and skill. Your memories bring us wisdom and we respect the things you say. But the bison have moved away to places where we cannot follow them. We still hunt, and the meat of the deer and the elk and the bears is rich and tasty, and their skins warm us in the winter. Times have changed. Even when we hunted the bison, we gathered wild plants for food, and now we have more of them to sustain us throughout the cold months. The old life was hard, and few grandfathers reached your years."

"Grandfathers!" A young voice spoke up. It was Rabbit Ears, cautious and respectful, for he had not yet earned the right to speak. "It's true that you are wiser than we in things of the hunt." (Some people laughed, for Rabbit Ears' bad luck in the hunt was well known.) "But life is changing for the better. The corn harvest will be more and better each year. It cannot run away and hide from us as the herds do. If we take care of it, it will take care of us. Don't you remember how good the hot corn cakes tasted last winter when the meat was all gone?" The people murmured approval because all knew of the fine crop in Rabbit Ears' farming patch.

This was not a new discussion. It went on constantly between the hunters of the old ways and the harvesters of the new. Wasn't there some way, Wonders wondered, for both ways to be combined? Grandfather was so wise. Surely, he understood the ways the People's lives were changing. Did he really want to return to the hunting days, or did he just want people to listen to him more appreciatively?

She fell asleep on her mat of woven bulrushes with the moon shining over the valley and the voices of her band murmuring around the fire, her head full of questions.

⌒

The next morning, everybody was up before dawn, for there was much work to do. Some men went off to the cornfields, women and girls to gather amaranth and sunflower seeds, boys to hunt rabbits. Grandfather was making new darts from deer bones, while other old men were repairing tool handles and weapons. Two old women were sewing pieces of leather into bags and pouches for meal and small seeds. Rabbit Ears was making the sandals of strong yucca fibers prized by everybody. Wonders took a turn at the grinding stones and sorted seeds in the flat sorting baskets. She worked with a stone scraper to clean the fat from the fresh deerskin and washed out the deer's stomach and intestines for containers, while she kept an eye on Baby Brother. She carefully avoided suggestions that she work on baskets.

But she was curious about her new basket, which she hoped would be her last. Would it hold water? She slipped away to find out.

No one else was at the river. She squatted on her favorite rock, soaked her new basket, and filled it with water. She lifted it up and waited. No water squirted out. So far, so good. She sat in the sun with the basket on her lap and smiled. At last she had done it, made a perfect . . . Suddenly, her left knee felt cold. Wet. The basket was leaking, slowly. She sighed. Frustration! What had she done wrong this time? Enough! No more caring about baskets for her.

As she thought about her problem, she noticed the little clay ball her baby brother had made the day before. She picked it up and saw that the sun had dried the outside. The hole her brother had punched with his fist was still wet, and it was half-filled with water. She poured the water out and, using a sharp piece of stone, began scraping the wet clay from the inside of the ball. She shaped it like a half-gourd and smoothed the sides both inside and out. She filled it with water and set it carefully on the sun-warmed rock before returning to camp.

All that afternoon as she worked around the camp, she thought about the little clay pot by the river. She remembered that Grandfather had told about a clay pot he had seen once carried by a man from the south. It was hard and light and painted with black designs. But he didn't know how it had been made. She imagined her own pot smooth and dry and hard. Maybe she could paint designs on it, and she began imagining what they might be. How surprised Grandfather would be! The pot was not as heavy as stone, nor as fragile as gourd, and unlike a basket it had taken only a minute to make. And it wouldn't leak! Why had no one of the People thought of that before?

⌐⌐

Finally, the afternoon sun turned red and dipped behind the western mesa. Wonders could wait no longer. She had told no one about the clay pot. Tonight, she would be the first one to go to the river for water. With a basket under her arm, she raced off.

There on the rock by the river's edge was the clay pot, just as she had left it. It was hard and dry. She poured more water into it. No leaks! She dropped her basket and ran back to camp.

She went to where Grandfather was working and tried to remember her manners. Almost bursting with eagerness, she stayed as quiet as she could until he looked up and acknowledged her. "Grandfather, please come to the river and let me show you something," she said more calmly than she felt. With a reluctant smile, he put down his tools and followed her. "I have a special surprise for you." Her words were loud and rapid, not the most respectful way to speak with the elders.

The little pot sat dry and smooth in the fading light. Wonders picked it up and held it out to Grandfather. "Look! Isn't it wonderful?"

"Huh! That lump of clay? What's so wonderful about it?"

"Grandfather, watch." She filled it with clean water and offered him a drink. "I've made a new type of pot, better than a basket!"

Grandfather began to laugh. "Now look," he told her. "Look again at your fine pot. It's all wet again. And the top, where it is driest—see how it is beginning to crack? It's no good." And with a twist of his hands, he broke the little pot in half. Wonders stared in disbelief.

⌒

Grandfather sat down on the rock next to Wonders. He held the pieces of the pot in his hands, turning them over and over as he spoke.

"Granddaughter, this is a good effort, but not the first. Whenever our people have tried to make clay pots before, they always crumble and break. I told you about the pot I saw once long ago, but I don't know what made it hard and whole. Maybe some day we'll find out the secret. But for now they don't work for us.

"Long ago our people learned to use the gourds that grow everywhere in the fall for scooping, carrying, storing water and seeds and dried meat. We use them for lots of things. But they are fragile and break easily. Our hunters use bags made from different parts of animals, as you know. But since we learned to weave baskets, so many different kinds of them, and saw how light and strong they can be, we're glad to have them. Yes, I miss the old days, but I know the time we spend in the valley is important and the baskets have made a great difference in the ways we do things. But clay pots? I don't think so. Not yet, anyway. But you ask questions all the time and wonder about many things. Keep on asking about clay pots and maybe you'll find out the secret."

The old man walked away, shaking his head. Wonders just sat on the rock staring at the pieces of broken clay. There must be some way. If the people of the south could keep their pots hard, how did they do it? She remembered the clay in the winter fire pit that they plastered over the stones. That clay was so hard! If she put a pot in the fire, what would happen to it? That was something she could try. And in the winter camp there were so many other people, maybe some of them knew about clay pots. She remembered Grandfather's last words to her and excitement began to fill her mind.

~

While she was thinking these things, Wonders had scooped up a large handful of clay from the riverbank. She started molding it with her hands. There was a hard lump inside. She rinsed off the mud.

It was something strange. A whitish slice of stone, or maybe bone. It had a hole in the middle and lines around the outside edge that looked as if they had been carved. What could it be? She would show it to Grandfather. Perhaps he might know what it was.

Wonders shivered. It was getting cold. The moon was rising over the ridge, bathing the valley in silver light and making the ripples in the river sparkle.

She tucked the carved bone in the little leather pouch hanging from her belt, filled her water basket, and ran back to camp.

3

Trade and Terror (1300 AD)

WILLOW CARRIED THE WATER pot on her shoulder, nestled between her ear and her supporting hand. Like all of Mother's pots, this one was light and strong and painted with black and white patterns. She hurried happily, eager to show off her new treasure.

"Mother," she called, as she approached the low houses straggling around one of the several courtyards of the village. Mother was standing in the doorway talking with Grandmother and the two other elderly women twining yucca fibers into cord. She looked up smiling, took the water pot from her daughter, and set it down by the doorway.

Willow loosened the sash that belted the cotton tunic tied over one shoulder and gathered about her waist. She drew out of its folds a little clay jar. Its fat little belly and narrow neck flared out at the top like the blossom of a flower. It was painted with green and yellow and black designs showing a rabbit, a corn plant and a rain cloud. Mother turned it around in her hands admiring the workmanship and passed it on to the other women. The little rabbit looked so comical they all laughed.

"Where did this come from? How did you get it?" she asked.

"I traded for it." Willow felt important. She had made a good exchange. "One of the girls down by the creek had gotten it from somewhere else, I don't know where."

"What did you trade?" asked Mother. Glancing at Willow's bare neck, she knew. "Your turquoise necklace—and the pendant of the Old Bone Bead? That's a gift from the Ancestors that your grandmother entrusted to your care! It's not something to trade!"

Grandmother, holding the jar that had delighted her a moment earlier, looked upset and very sad. But she said nothing.

Willow realized with a shock that she had betrayed a trust. A sinking feeling gripped her stomach as she defended herself. "That's just an old piece of bone. The other girl said it looked interesting and she would only trade the little pot for both it and the turquoise. We can always get more turquoise. Isn't this jar the most handsome you have ever seen?"

Grandfather stopped working at his loom nearby and came over to see what was happening. He admired the jar extravagantly. "This is clay from Mother Earth, combined with the skill, spirit and imagination of the maker. That is good. But it's no substitute for the caring and wisdom of the Ancestors that come to us through what you call 'just an old bone.'" He hurled it to the ground. The jar didn't break but bounced into the basket among the coils of yucca cord Grandmother had been working on. He turned and stomped angrily back to his loom where he was weaving a fine piece of cotton cloth.

⌐

Willow felt herself shrinking into the ground. But then the dog lying in the doorway leaped up barking, joined by others nearby, raising a great hullabaloo.

A line of six men passed through the courtyard at a steady trot. Each carried on his back a burden basket suspended from his forehead by a sturdy strap. The baskets were heaped high with cotton, round blobs of soft white stuff. The men had set out several days ago for one of the southern villages where the people cultivated cotton in their irrigated fields. They had taken baskets of piñon nuts to exchange for the loads they were carrying

The last in line was Two Feathers, Willow's older brother. This was his first trading trip. He looked hungry, tired, dirty. His skin and his cotton loincloth were streaked with sweat and dust. His eyes were shining, as he jerked his chin and flapped his fingers toward his family. Before he could speak to them, he had to report with the others to the Village Council in the central plaza. He kept up with the older men's tireless trot, but Willow could see that he staggered with exhaustion.

Father came out of the doorway from which he had watched the arrival. Willow could tell from his expression that he was glad that his son had returned safely. But his words were gruff. "Now that he has seen someplace else, he'd better settle down to help with the corn fields and the hunting and the care of our people here. We don't want him to become a *gadabout* like his grandfather." And he walked off toward the welcoming gathering of the Council of Elders, for he was one of them.

Grandfather snorted and yanked viciously at the cotton thread in his hand, but said nothing. Grandmother went back to twisting and twining the yucca fibers into the endless amounts of cord needed every day. Gradually her friends resumed their conversation.

～

Mother motioned with her head toward the doorway. Willow picked up the water jar and poured its contents into the much larger container just inside. She replaced the lid and the gourd dippers on top.

The room was small and neatly kept, one of three the family shared with the grandparents. During warm weather, they spent most of the time outside, eating and sleeping under the brush arbor sheltering the fireplace and grinding stones beside the door.

The water stayed cooler inside the house. The jars of corn meal and dried beans were protected from insects and mice here. Blankets and hides were hung on poles suspended from the roof beams, and woven rush sleeping mats were rolled up against the walls. The small hearth, now cold, warmed the room and cooked the food when the weather was stormy and when the icy winds whipped down from the mountains. A small opening opposite the doorway let the smoke out—sometimes. A deerskin, now pegged up by the door, kept the cold drafts from entering.

Willow peeked into the storeroom. It was piled high with the things that made up their lives. Ears of dried corn were stacked along the walls. Beans of different kinds overflowed baskets and large pottery containers. Strings of dried squash, pumpkins, wild onions and roots hung from the roof beams. Baskets of cotton waited to be spun and woven into cloth. Farming tools, bows and arrows, and baskets of fine-grained stone and obsidian to be shaped into knives and scrapers and arrowheads were heaped on the floor. Containers for needles and awls and flutes, jars with pieces of turquoise and shells for jewelry sat in the corners. Some hides and cotton blankets hung from poles. The dog lived in this room, eating any mice or rats that strayed in. Willow had heard of some people who kept in their storerooms tame snakes that grew big and fat from the mice they ate. She hadn't seen any, but they sounded interesting.

Grandmother had built the house with the help of other women, for building houses was women's work. The men, in charge of spiritual life, built the kivas. They had mixed masses of mud with charcoal down by the creek and lugged many basketfuls to the site. There the women poured the walls, one layer at a time, adding another layer when the earlier one was dry and hard. They had dragged roof beams from the mountains and set them in place, then piled smaller sticks and brush and lots more mud on top to make the house strong and snug. Willow had helped smooth and plaster the walls and floors with more mud, which was a job even small children could do.

Willow liked to go into the third room. It smelled wonderful. Many bunches of dried herbs and roots hung from the ceiling. Grandmother was known as a healer. She had often taken Willow along to help gather and carry the various plants, and to learn about them. One area where the healing plants were particularly plentiful was on a ridge a little way upstream. A number of circular dips in the ground held rainwater and snowmelt longer than most places nearby. Grandmother often told her, "People used to live here in houses built partly underground like our kivas. They are long gone now."

But now, Grandmother, once so strong and energetic, ached in all her joints. She could barely hobble around. No longer was she able to grind corn or carry water or crouch down to tend the cooking fire. She spent her days twining yucca fibers into cord, something she could still do. Now she watched over the children and told them stories from the ancestors and the tales passed down from them, and taught them to twine and knot the yucca strings. Willow loved her dearly and felt distressed that she had hurt her by trading the gift of the ancestors.

〜

Would Mother scold her some more? To distract her, Willow asked her a question that had bothered her for a longtime.

"Why does Father seem so angry with Grandfather sometimes? Isn't trading a good thing for our people? Isn't it? Isn't it good that Two Feathers is becoming a trader too?"

Mother sighed, "Grandfather has filled your head with stories of the places and people he has seen. He brags about how he could trot along all day across deserts and mountains with a heavy burden on his back and only a handful of dried corn to eat. He talks about the things he carried from one village to another—the seeds, shells, salt, bright colored feathers, copper bells, arrow points, dried buffalo meat, spindle whorls, clay pipes and whistles, bone needles and flutes, woven sashes and feather blankets, turquoise beads, information and news, songs and stories, and so much more. Once he even brought a live parrot from someplace far to the south. We liked the many new goods and ideas from other places he brought us, and he was well respected for them. The trading was all so romantic and exciting, and like the old stories of Kokopelli, he was welcomed almost everywhere.

But he doesn't talk about the other side of it. Your father's father was a friend and trading partner. Together, they were away from the village for months at a time. They weren't here to help with the harvest or to work on the kivas or for the important ceremonials that show respect for the Unseen Ones who protect and care for the people. When they were needed, they weren't here. Then your father's father was killed in an ambush. Your grandfather ran away safely, but never went back to care for his friend's body with the proper prayers and rituals. All their trading goods were lost. Your father's mother died from sorrow soon afterwards.

"Your father has spent his life trying to stay with the people here and help them in every way his father did not. And now he's afraid Two Feathers will go off and never return. Grandfather weaves now because he is too old for such travels, but he is encouraging Two Feathers to seek adventure."

Willow, always charmed by Grandfather's stories, had never though of it that way. As she was pondering what Mother had said, another hubbub erupted. She heard Grandmother's voice shouting at one of the turkeys that had escaped from its pen and was pecking around the dooryard. Its questing beak banged down on the paw of the dog snoozing in the doorway. The dog leaped up with a howl, chased the turkey around, chomped down on it with his jaws, while nearby kids and people yelled and whacked him with sticks to make him let it go. When the dog finally dropped the turkey, it was dead.

What a shame! There were other turkeys in the pens near the house, fed and tended for their luxuriant feathers. Willow picked up the bloody carcass and started plucking off and sorting the feathers. Little Brother woke up from his nap in the shade near Grandmother and gathered up loose feathers scattered around. Some would be saved for ceremonies or decorations, some would help arrows fly straight. Most would be soaked, split, and twined around long yucca cords, which would then be woven into soft, light blankets. It was a long and tedious process with which Willow had helped often. The blankets were warm and welcome in cold weather.

Mother cut up the turkey for stew and tossed it into a large clay pot. She poured in some water, added a couple of handfuls of dry beans, some fresh roots and wild onions. She set the pot on the three clay supports over the cooking fire. Grandmother could easily feed the fire from where she sat with sticks from the nearby pile, and she and Grandfather could tend Little Brother for a while.

"Come on, Willow. Let's get some clay," Mother invited. Willow picked up a basket and followed her gladly. They walked through the small village straggling along the curve in the creek, past the pit where yucca leaves were soaked and pounded to loosen the strong fibers, and on upstream to their favorite clay deposit. The water felt cool on their bare feet, and Willow liked the contrasts between the squishy mud and the hard surfaces of the rocks along the way.

Willow liked the process of making pottery. It started with the scattering of sacred corn meal and prayers to Mother Earth before they scooped out handfuls of the gray clay. Then there was the kneading of the hard clay into a smooth dough, and the building of the pots and bowls, cups and jugs with long, soft coils of it. Then the careful smoothing of the sides, inside and out, and the time spent patiently waiting while the pots dried in the sun. Then more polishing the surfaces with smooth river stones. Some of the cooking pots were roughed up on the surface with corncobs so they would hold the heat better and not slip out of the cooks' hands. Painting designs with yucca brushes was always a joyful time. More polishing, and then the all-important baking in a covered fire until the clay glowed and became hard. Willow's pots were still crude and lopsided and often broke, but Mother was a good teacher, reminding her constantly that it took years to learn the ways of the clay. Making pottery is a sacred task, she insisted. Shaping Mother Earth for human needs requires respect and special rituals. But Willow realized that almost every aspect of their lives was also sacred, each with prayers and ceremonies to bring the blessings of the Unseen Ones.

As they bent over the clay deposit, Mother suddenly lifted her head. "Something is happening at the village!" Now Willow could hear it too, a lot of shouting and screaming. She moved out into the creek bed to see around the curve. But Mother pushed past her, scrambling up the slippery bank, running through the piñon and juniper trees toward the village, calling for Father and the baby. Though Willow wanted to run away and hide, she forced herself to race after Mother.

Some women and children burst through the trees, nearly knocking them down. "Run," they screamed. "Hide! Save yourselves! They are burning our homes. They will kill us!"

The women pushed Mother and Willow ahead of them, away from the village. Willow caught her foot and was thrown forward, sliding headfirst into the arroyo. Something heavy fell on top of her, wedging her between two large rocks. Everything went black

A while later, Willow was aware of someone tugging her arm. "Willow, child, are you all right?" It was Mother's voice. "Willow, can you hear me? Wake up! I can't pull you out all by myself."

Slowly, the girl managed to twist herself around. She tried to clamber out of her rocky prison, but one foot was stuck tight. She wiggled and tugged at it with no success, until hands shifted one of the rocks so that she could free herself. Her head hurt, her foot hurt, her knees and elbows were bruised and bleeding.

More people gathered around. There was Two Feathers carrying her up the bank. Everything was quiet. The air hung heavy with smoke.

〜

As the little group limped home, Two Feathers explained what had happened. A bunch of strangers had rushed screaming into the village, chasing the women and old people away. They trapped many of the men in the kivas where they were working. Most of the others were far from their weapons. They ran through the houses, taking what they wanted and destroying much of the rest. They left as quickly as they had come, lugging whatever they could carry. Bags of ground corn meal, dried beans, cotton and feather blankets, baskets, small tools and weapons, turquoise jewelry. They had smashed pots, scattered cooking fires, knocked down brush arbors, killed dogs and turkeys, set fire to some of the houses, tossed burning sticks into the community granary where a large store of corn was saved for emergencies.

They had wounded several people and killed two. One of the latter was a brother of Willow's father. He had been a fine hunter until he had broken a leg that never healed. properly. After that, he had become a carver, well known for his beautiful bone whistles, pipes and flutes.

The other victim was—Grandmother! She couldn't run. She couldn't fight. But she stood up brave and strong, shouting at the invaders, until one of them bashed in her head with his war club.

Grandfather had scooped up Little Brother and run to safety. An arrow had slashed through the skin of Father's arm. He had wound strips of cotton cloth around it to stop the bleeding.

Willow gasped when she saw the damage. One whole block of houses was burning, and the roofs were falling in. The smell of corn burning in the granary filled the air. Her own family's house was intact, just as she had left it, except for Grandmother lying outside the door, her head in a pool of blood.

Two Feathers snatched up his bow and a handful of arrows and joined a group of men setting out to pursue the invaders. Laden with loot, they surely couldn't travel as fast as the lightly-armed warriors. But the men lost the trail and after a while came back dejected.

Meanwhile, under Father's direction, the people tried to absorb what had happened and start cleaning up the mess. The fires were extinguished, wreckage picked up or repaired as much as possible. The injured were tended, the dead mourned.

Grandfather was devastated. How could he live without the woman who had shared his life, whom he had abandoned to her fate? Mother was stricken. How could she live without the love and council of her mother? They carefully picked up the body, wrapped it in her sleeping mat and placed it in the room she and Grandfather had shared. After proper prayers and rituals, they would prepare a shallow grave, block up the doorway, and leave her to eternal rest. Then they both hacked off the long hair they were so proud of as a sign of mourning.

Willow, too, was devastated. Her grandmother, her best friend, teacher, comforter, confidant. How she would miss her! What would Grandmother say to her if she were here now? Since she was a practical woman, she would probably remind Willow that whatever the circumstances, people have to eat.

The pot was still sitting on its clay supports, though the fire under it had burned down. Willow stirred up the coals and added small sticks until the flames burst out again. She added water to the simmering stew, poured in handfuls of corn meal to thicken it, a little salt and some herbs from the jars beside the fireplace. She stirred it with the carved wooden spoon and set the scooping gourds nearby. It smelled good, but nobody seemed hungry.

Her head still ached while she cleaned off her injuries from the fall. Then a terrible thought occurred to her. Was *she* responsible for Grandmother's death? She had traded away the Gift of the Ancestors. Were they angry? Had they sent the raiders to punish her? Was this the penalty for betraying the trust? Her stomach churned up and tears rolled down her cheeks.

The sun glinted off something in the basket where Grandmother had been coiling the yucca cord. Willow reached over and picked up the little yellow and green jar that had delighted Grandmother earlier today. It seemed a lifetime ago. How Grandmother had laughed at the perky figures painted on it.

Hardly knowing what she was doing, her thoughts filled with Grandmother, Willow gathered up a bunch of small, brightly colored feathers for prayers, a necklace made of shells from waters far away, a piece of polished turquoise for the beauty of earth and sky, a flake of obsidian for the tools the Ancient Ones had taught the people to make, a few kernels of corn and some beans for the journey, and a sprig of dried herb that renewed life and health. She put them all in the little jar and stoppered it with a piece of corncob, the bearer of food. She dug a hole in the floor near Grandmother's head, lined it with dry grass, and buried the little jar in memory of Grandmother and to keep their spirits connected. Mother had already placed beside Grandmother her favorite black-and-white bowl that Grandfather had brought her long ago from a great stone city far to the west.

⌒

As they sat around the fire under the brush arbor that evening, men and women, friends and relatives came to sit with them and help them mourn their loss. Grandfather looked ancient, sitting hunched, sunk into himself. Father was gray and exhausted. Mother stared off into the distance, moaning softly to herself, rocking back and forth with Little Brother clutched in her arms. Two Feathers, still dirty and sweaty from his trip, seemed to have revived the most. He even nodded, "Good stew," to Willow, a compliment that on other occasions would have made her glow with pleasure. She was glad she couldn't see what *she* looked like this evening.

Again and again, the talk turned to what was on everybody's mind. How can we protect our village from future raids like this one?

Build a wall around the village, some said. But the houses straggled all along a bend in the creek. There were no natural defenses. Invaders could come from anywhere.

Keep warriors standing guard, watching out for hostile strangers all the time. But too few men were available to watch from too many places, and they were needed for other tasks.

Build mutual defense coalitions with the friendly villages in the area. Friends from some of them had come to help clean up the damage. All of them shared the same concern. There should be some way for all of them to help prepare for trouble.

Grandfather said nothing, but Father spoke in his place. Grandfather, the trader, he reminded his listeners, had visited villages and large towns where the houses were built on top of one another. There were no outside doors to the bottom rooms. Ladders that could be pulled up in times of emergency provided the only way people could reach the upper floors where they lived and worked. Such a system would have saved lives and goods stolen from them today.

Two Feathers spoke up. Generally, he kept silent in the presence of his elders, but today was different. "Grandfather has told us," he reminded, "about strong towns he has visited, set on high places with rock walls and heaped up houses where no strangers can get in unless invited. We can't build such a place here, but a little upstream is the rocky ridge we all know. The sides are steep, there is plenty of stone for building and springs of water on top as well as in the creek below. We could farm on the flat lands all around, just as we do here. Grandfather told me of his dream, of building a town on that ridge with a large plaza surrounded by houses built up to three or four levels all around. There would be rooms for storage, for kivas, for dances and ceremonies, and the entryways from outside could be guarded easily. It would be hard work to build such a place, but perhaps other nearby villages would join us."

Grandfather grunted and nodded his head. "Well spoken, Grandson. That would be a good place to live."

And the talk went on and on, while bodies grew cold and wounds healed and the firelight cast its glow on the weary people.

⌒

The next morning, Mother and some of the other women went to the creek to gather baskets of mud to seal up the door to the room where Grandmother lay amidst the fragrance of the herbs suspended from the roof beams. Willow was left to tend the fire, grind some corn and watch Little Brother. She still felt numb. She hardly noticed the beautiful day with some trees beginning to turn yellow, or the way Little Brother's head had been handsomely flattened in back by the cradleboard he had outgrown, or the many colors of the corn grains she was grinding, or the way the sun shone on the house walls nearby. Sadness weighed down her spirit and tears dripped off her nose into the corn meal. If only she had not traded away . . .

"Willow, stand up!" Grandfather's voice had its old ring, even though there were dark hollows around his eyes and his wrinkles seemed deeper. As she rose, she felt something slip over her head and a familiar weight thumped against her chest. The ancient bead, the Gift of the Ancestors! Grandfather was looking deep into her eyes. She noticed that his turquoise and eagle claw pendant was missing. Had he traded it for the bone bead?

She felt his arms tighten around her shoulders and wrapped hers around his waist. In this strong embrace, she felt his love and forgiveness, and that of Grandmother and of all the ancestors seeping into her, and her tears flowed freely.

The old bone scrunched between them. Willow knew she would never again betray its trust.

Part II

The Great Pecos Pueblo

*B*uilt gradually in the 1300s, the fortified pueblo first known as Cicuye *(The Stone Place), and later as* Pecos, *gathered together people from the small outlying communities. The town on the steep-sided ridge was easy to defend. Water and farmlands were close by. Stone for building and wood for fires were plentiful. The pass between the Rio Grande pueblos and the Great Plains opened out in both directions. Pecos soon became known for its extensive trade with all sorts of people, for its abundant harvests and for its brave warriors. The Spanish explorers of 1540 estimated a population of about 2,000 people, but the numbers gradually diminished until the final handful migrated to Jemez Pueblo in 1838.*

N

4. Pueblo and Plains (1550 AD)
Buffalo hunting plains tribes gathered at Pecos each fall to barter hides,
dried meat, bones, tanned skins, hoofs and horns, other animal products,
and many other items from the plains people and beyond. Especially
desired were captives. In exchange, they received corn, beans, pottery,
cotton and feather blankets, turquoise, parrot feathers, and countless
other items from the Rio Grande area and points farther south and west.
How did people as different from each other, the wandering hunters and
the settled farmers, get along together?

5. "*Cristo* is Here" (1625 AD)
The first Spanish settlers arrived in the Rio Grande area in 1598. Santa
Fe was founded in 1610. Franciscan missionaries were assigned to
many of the pueblos to build mission churches and to serve and convert
the people. Some of the missionaries used force and intimidation
and destruction of the pueblo sacred objects. Others used allure and
encouragement. One of the latter was Father Andrés Júarez who served at
Pecos for 13 years (1621–1634), completing the great church building and
defending the Pecos inhabitants from abuses by the colonial government.

6. After the Spanish Left (1681 AD)
In 1680, the pueblo people throughout the Rio Grande area, angered
by the continuing abuses of the civil government and mission policies,
and struggling from the effects of severe drought and the heavy tributes
demanded, drove the Spanish colonists out of New Mexico.
Their charismatic leader, Popé, who had united all the diverse pueblos for
the first time, soon became dictatorial, insisting that all traces of Spanish
culture, the good as well as the bad, should be destroyed.
This caused considerable conflict within and among the often-squabbling
pueblos, and Popé was soon replaced by other leaders. Though Pecos
warriors helped drive out the settlers, their leaders were among the
supporters of Don Diego de Vargas when he brought back
the Spanish colony twelve years later.

7. Was it a Bear? (1760 AD)

How does humor help people survive tough times? The *koshare*, the sacred clowns, are a traditional element in Pueblo life, in their many guises making fun of people and events, diminishing stress with raucous laughter. Agustín Guiche was a real person. The bear—or was it a bear?— really killed him. Bishop Tamarón, the victim of the burlesque, recounted the story with delight and wrote an account of it to share with friends. This event has passed into the folklore of Pecos.

8. Departure—Where To? (1838 AD)

Only a handful of people were left at Pecos Pueblo by this time. The community could no longer sustain itself. The valley was changing. New settlers were developing farms and ranches, new communities emerging, and Anglo traders were passing through with their huge freight wagons on the "Santa Fe Trail." Where should this last remnant of the once-great pueblo go, and why? And how did they feel about leaving their ancestral home?

4

Pueblos and Plains (1550 AD)

"TEYAS COMING!" The voice of the watcher on the high point of the pueblo echoed over the busy plaza. Other voices took up the cry. People dropped whatever they were doing and rushed to the rooftops to look.

Flame scrambled up the ladders along with the others. Way down the valley, little black dots were moving, coming into view. The Buffalo People were on the move. They would set up their tipis in the open field below the pueblo, for trade, for talk, for feasting, for fun.

"Why do they have to come NOW?" Her father's voice beside her was grumpy. "Just when the crops are ready and we need every pair of hands to help with the harvest. Now we'll spend days with these strangers, wasting time in frivolities. They're prickly, unpredictable people, and if we offend them somehow they'll burn our cornfields and steal our children . . ."

"Don't be so grumpy!" her mother scolded her father. "You know they come here every year about this time. And we still manage to bring in the harvest. These strangers bring us dried buffalo meat and warm buffalo robes for our beds and lots of other things they have made and traded from far away. They bring new ideas and news and stories of other places and people. It's years since they have stolen any of our children. Maybe among the ones they bring we can find a new son for Broken Wing." She shifted Baby Brother on her hip. Her voice was eager and excited.

"Harrumph!" growled Father, setting down the basket of beans he was carrying. There was a twinkle in his eye. Flame looked at Mother and they both laughed. The same conversation was repeated every year, and they knew that Father was as eager to welcome the visitors as they were

Flame's spirit soared as she breathed in the cool air and looked out over the valley. It was a beautiful day! The early snow on the mountains gleamed in the sunshine. The trees near the river glowed golden with changing leaves. The early-planted farm patches along the creek shone tawny, later-planted ones showed varying shades of green and yellow. Orange pumpkins were scattered among them.

Here on the rooftop, the turkeys gobbled in their pens beside the windbreak. Ears of corn were spread out on mats to finish drying. They were yellow, white, red, black, speckled—corn, the giver of life. Beans brown, white, red-and-white speckled, were heaped on other mats waiting to be cleaned, sorted and stored in pottery jars. Yellow squash and pumpkins, cut in chunks, were drying in the sun. Later, they would be strung on yucca cords and hung from rafters in the storerooms. A basket of piñon nuts was also awaiting attention. The harvest had begun, but there was much, much more to gather and prepare for the long winter months.

⌒

Down below in the great plaza surrounded by terraced house blocks three and four stories high, people were gathering in clusters, talking, preparing. Many things had to be done before the Teyas arrived, and they all knew their tasks.

With a mixture of excitement and anxiety, for she was always a little afraid of these tall, fierce strangers, Flame grabbed her wood-gathering strap and slid down the ladder to the plaza. There she joined a group of other girls who would collect as much firewood as they could, for there wouldn't be much time over the next few days, and the Teyas would quickly pick up everything that would burn. Two armed warriors accompanied each group of girls. Though the Teyas were coming in peace, they weren't to be trusted completely.

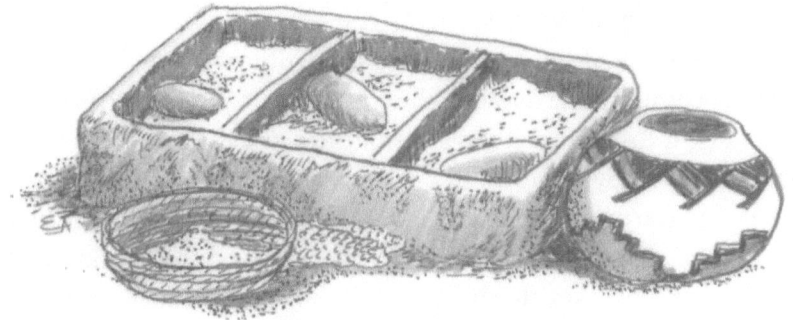

As she left the plaza, Flame could see Mother settling down behind the grinding stones to prepare quantities of corn meal. Broken Wing was bringing jar after jar of water from the spring to fill the large containers just inside the doorway. When she returned, she would join Mother at the grinding stones. She could see Grandmother adding more beans and herbs to the pot of stew simmering over the cooking fire beside her doorway and watching Baby Brother who, for once, was sitting quietly chewing on a piece of squash. Boys were on the rooftops checking supplies of arrows, spears and stones in case the visitors should turn hostile. Grandfather was already in the central kiva with the other elders planning the welcome, while young runners—her brother Bead Maker among them—were popping out of the kivas to carry word of the approach of the Teyas to nearby pueblos. Other people were picking up looms and blankets, tools, pots, mats, hides, pipes, beads, corn, clay, herbs, gaming pieces, weapons, almost everything except the grinding stones and cooking fires and putting them in the storerooms. It wouldn't do to let the visitors see how much the Cicuye people had.

By the time Flame returned with her third load of firewood, the plaza looked bare. The terraces were neat and the people, talking animatedly, were gathering on the rooftops and terraces. Even the dogs sniffing around seemed to feel the excitement in the air.

Flame climbed the ladders to join the others on the rooftop. The Teyas were coming close now and she could see them clearly. The warriors strode along in front and at the sides of the procession, their spears and leather shields ready to protect the women with their baskets and babies. The captives were bent under large burdens. The big wolf-dogs hauled heavy bundles tied to the poles they dragged behind them. The children scampered among them all with their own small burdens on their backs. They flowed into the trading field in apparent confusion.

Flame never tired of watching them make camp. The loads were set down. Almost instantly, poles were set up, skin tipi covers fastened around them, fires started, food brought out. No confusion: everything was well organized with an efficiency from constant practice. Flame wondered what it would be like to move around all the time. She had always lived in these solid stone structures around the plaza that enclosed and protected people. The Teyas followed the buffalo; she was rooted like the corn.

"Here they come!" Mother gestured with her chin. Flame saw four men approaching the narrow main entrance to the pueblo. They were taller than the pueblo men, lean and angular, and walked with a loose-jointed stride. Most of the people Flame knew were shorter, more rounded and compact, shaped by their different kinds of work and living conditions. The strangers carried their weapons and painted shields.

Flame's skin always prickled with excitement at these welcoming ceremonies. Father stood on the rooftop on one side of the entrance. Beside him, Toba, who had come from far to the south, blew on a large white shell with a shiny pink inside. It made a loud wailing sound that echoed over the valley. Hopping Bird, brought as a captive from one of the plains tribes by the Teyas several years ago, called out to the visitors in their own language. His voice was loud and clear.

"Strangers, who are you? Why do you come to our town of Cicuye, The Stone Place? Do you come in peace or war?" Flame didn't understand the words but she knew their meaning.

One of the visitors responded in the Cicuye language. "We are the Teyas, from the eastern plains. We follow the buffalo. We come to trade with the people of Cicuye. We come in peace." And each of the men laid down his weapons and shield on the rock beside the entrance and touched the earth with his hand in the universal sign for peace. The pueblo warriors on the opposite roof by the entrance ceremonially put down their spears, as Toba's shell wailed again.

⌐⌐

As the Teyas entered the plaza, they were greeted by the pounding of deep pueblo drums and the shrill notes of bird-bone flutes. A double row of picked dancers with gourd rattles in their hands escorted the visitors to the waiting elders. They were dressed in their finest kilts and sandals, turquoise jewelry around their necks, and painted cotton robes draped over their shoulders.

Flame slid down the ladders to ground level because she wanted to watch the proceedings more closely. But she missed her footing and fell on her face at the feet of one of the visitors. As she looked up, she saw sturdy calf-high moccasins, a soft deerskin breech clout, a bear claw necklace, two feathers hanging from a thick braid, skin shiny with grease rubbed on to protect it from sun and wind. A long face looked down and laughed at her. She scrambled to her feet, red with shame, and hid behind other watchers.

Grandfather was offering a prayer of welcome and scattering sacred corn pollen. Other elders made long speeches and the visitors responded, with Hopping Bird translating back and forth. Grandmother was one of the women who brought out ceremonial gifts: a beautiful pottery jar full of fresh spring water, a bowl of corn meal and a cotton blanket painted with designs of flying birds. In turn, the visitors presented a fine buffalo robe with head and tail still attached. Then the drums and flutes and deep voices of the singing men resounded through the plaza, as the dancers danced the precise, traditional steps of the ritual welcome dance.

Finally, the elders took the Teyas down into one of the kivas for more talk, for smoking, for feasting, while the rest of the people went back to their tasks. Flame watched to see if any of the Teyas would pop out of the hatches like prairie dogs out of their holes. Grandfather had told her that "open sky people" were always nervous in the underground ceremonial rooms. Therefore, he said, it was important to host them down in them, but Flame wasn't quite sure why.

⌒

The next day was for visiting. All day long, groups of people went back and forth between the stone pueblo on the ridge and the Teya camp below. They were looking, getting acquainted, revisiting folks they had known previous years, sharing food and skills, conversing in mixtures of signs and the few words of each other's language they knew. It was lively and fun.

Several groups of women and girls stopped at Grandmother's house-block. As women do everywhere, they examined each other's clothes—the sturdy cotton garments of the Cicuye women, the soft buckskin dresses adorned with shells and fringes of the Teyas. They were particularly curious about the tame turkeys and the feather blankets Grandmother had made. They looked at cooking and household arrangements, the sleeping quarters and small children.

The Teya women seemed nervous on the ladders that connected the various levels of the pueblo. Flame lured a couple of them all the way to the top to see the turkeys in their pens and then had to help them down. How they laughed when they saw one of the pueblo dogs scampering up and down the ladders. Broken Wing showed them how easily she could climb the ladders with a water jug on her head. When one of the Teya women tried it, she spilled the water and fell off the ladder, to great teasing from her friends.

Meanwhile, Grandmother had set some of them at the grinding stones, showing them how each of the three stones crushed the corn kernels into meal of different consistencies, and invited them to go to work. But soon the Teyas protested, "Too hard, too much work." Mother showed them how she made her pottery and invited a couple of the visitors to paint designs on a new pot with a yucca brush, but they were too shy.

When the visitors peered into the rooms, Flame showed them the rolled-up sleeping mats and the blankets hanging on the horizontal pole. She offered them a drink from the big water jar just inside the door using the split gourds that served as cups. She let them run their fingers through the corn meal and beans in storage jars securely stoppered to keep out bugs and hungry mice. They admired the deer antlers attached to the wall with belts and moccasins hanging from the tines, and the niche holding the handsome pot in which some of the family treasures were kept. Their tipis had no solid walls!

Flame explained how the dark inner rooms were used for storage, and how the walls and floors were plastered with light-colored clay that reflected the light. But when she showed how she cleaned the floor with a brush broom, the women laughed. With gestures they told her that when their floors got dirty, they simply picked up the tipis and moved somewhere else.

Grandmother had prepared a great stew of beans, corn and squash, with wild onions, herbs and rabbit meat. While she dished out samples in gourd bowls and pulled corncakes out of the ashes where they had been baking, the Cicuye women tried to explain their living conditions to the Teyas.

Grandmother was the head of the household. She and other women of the family built and maintained their rooms in the pueblo that were connected to all the others around the plaza. They gathered and broke up stones from the nearby ridges, set them into sturdy walls held together with mud from the creek, and plastered them all over with clay. ("Too hard, too much work!" exclaimed the visitors.) The rooms on the bottom layer were mostly for storage, reached by ladders through hatchways in the roofs.

In the rooms above the storerooms lived Grandmother, Grandfather and Broken Wing, their youngest daughter. Her husband had disappeared on a hunting trip and her small son had died when he fell off a ladder onto his head. Now that Hopping Bird had moved in with her, she seemed happier.

Flame lived on the top level with her mother, father and baby brother. Her older brother, Bead Maker, was being initiated into one of the kiva societies, a process that took many moons. He spent most of the time in the kiva, learning from the elders and serving them and the pueblo whatever their needs.

In the apartments on the other side of the building, facing away from the plaza, one of Grandmother's sisters lived with her large family. Broad terrace walkways surrounded each level where people lived and worked and visited with each other. They stayed inside only when it was dark or cold or windy. The rooftops were for turkeys and shared space for living. There the people could spread out their crops to dry, watch out over the countryside, and shoot arrows to repel possible invaders. The ladders could easily be pulled up in times of emergency; there were no entrances on the outside of the pueblo, and the narrow passageways into the plaza could easily be guarded. Their men were fierce warriors, productive farmers, traders who traveled far and wide, and leaders of the rich spiritual life that kept them connected with the ancestors and the Unseen Ones. Grandmother's two sons had moved in with their wives' families in other parts of the pueblo.

All this seemed very strange to the Teya women. They couldn't imagine living surrounded by stone walls, always in one place. They followed their men wherever the buffalo led them. Many of their men had several women as wives. The very idea of their men, who were hunters and warriors, grubbing in the ground tending corn plants, made them laugh. Yet each went away clutching a fine ear of corn as a gift.

Later, Flame and her mother, Broken Wing and some other women went to visit the Teya camp. The women there were ready for them. They invited the Cicuye women to set up a tipi and laughed when the poles kept falling down and they got tangled up in the hide covering. They demonstrated how to catch one of the big dogs and how to hold him while they hitched up the drag poles. But when the dog growled at them, the Cicuye women were afraid to approach him. The pueblo dogs were much smaller and not as fierce looking. When the Teya women invited Flame to ride n the basket attached to the poles and the dog sat down and refused to move, everybody laughed

They looked inside the tipis and saw everything not being used at the moment packed away in bags and rawhide containers. They were ready to move away to someplace else at a moment's notice. Dried meat or wild onions or various herbs were stored in some of the hard rawhide boxes that were decorated with painted designs and porcupine quills. Soft deerskin bags, with long fringes and decorations of shells and elks' teeth, stored clothes, extra moccasins, warm blankets. Pouches of decorated skins attached to their belts held their flint knives, scrapers, bone awls and needles, and coils of sinew for sewing always within reach. Flame wondered how the thin-skinned tipis could keep people warm in the howling storms of winter, and why rain didn't pour in through the smoke hole and drench the fire beneath, and what they ate when their meat was all gone.

Mother particularly admired the beautiful leatherwork, the tanned buckskin dresses and shirts, the buffalo skin moccasins and warm robes. They all oohed and aahed over a splendid baby carrier of soft buckskin attached to a wooden frame, and they oohed some more at the little baby peering out at them. The Teyas offered them a concoction of shredded dried buffalo meat mixed with fat, dried berries and herbs that tasted much better than it looked. This was their "hunger food" for when the buffalo were scarce. It gave them strength and courage, and it kept well in the leather bags without rotting.

The conical tipis were decorated with various designs on the lower parts and smoke-blackened toward the tops. Light seeped through during the daytimes; the fireplace was in the center and robes for seats and bedding were ranged around the edges. The thin walls leaned in toward the top, leaving nothing solid to lean against or to hold things. Flame appreciated how easily the tipi covering could be dismantled, folded up into a light package, and carried off to the next camp. She wondered what it would be like to live in such a place. She felt nervous and a little frightened at the thought.

All during that day, entranced, Flame watched the lively scene all around her, both inside and outside of the pueblo walls. Groups of men were sitting and talking, smoking stubby pipes, playing gambling games with marked pieces of bone, comparing tattoos and ornaments, laughing uproariously at some joke. Others were more serious, examining tools and weapons, looms and cornfields. Old men, elders of both communities, sat together observing all the activities, sharing an occasional comment. Women hustled about, tending to their tasks and young ones. Children clung to their mothers amidst the strangers, or peered from the cradles or shawls slung on the mothers' backs. Boys challenged each other with wild tests of skill, hurling spear-sticks through rolling hoops, shooting arrows at moving targets. Little girls admired dolls, some made of husk-clothed corncobs, others of stuffed and painted deerskin. Captives were lugging great loads of firewood, tending the dogs, hauling water from the springs in leather containers. Flame occasionally glimpsed her brother, Bead Maker, showing some Teyas how he ground, pierced and polished bits of shell, stone or bone for ornaments. The ancient bone bead Grandfather had entrusted to him gleamed white against his brown chest. He had deepened the faded carved lines, oiled and polished the bone until it shone. And of course, he and the other young men and women appraised each other with interest, seeking romance. Flame looked too, admiring the lean, lithe bodies and the confident expressions on the faces of the young Teya men.

Hopping Bird seemed to be everywhere, hobbling from group to group, translating, interpreting, explaining jokes and meanings, defusing tensions, his own good cheer infusing the spirit of the day. It was a wonderfully lively scene, but warriors on the rooftops watched everything carefully because the Cicuyes didn't really trust the Teyas and some of the elders of both communities were ready to intervene if quarrels got out of hand.

At sunset the light, one-sided Teya drums came out, and men and women started dancing around a central bonfire. Flame watched from the rooftop, her pulse throbbing with the rhythm of the drums. The Teyas bobbed and whirled, stamped and leaped in no particular pattern that she could identify. Each person seemed full of high spirits, dancing independently of the others. That seemed strange to Flame: The Cicuye dances were community prayers, for rain, for corn, for animals, for thanks for the harvest, the people moving together to the rhythm of the deep pueblo drums and the voices of the singers, their steps restrained and precise as handed down from the ancestors. Flame wanted to go closer, to maybe try the free dancing of the visitors, but the elders had forbidden the Cicuye girls from leaving the pueblo during the night. They still didn't really trust the Teyas.

⤿

The next day the trading started and continued for several days. People from nearby villages brought their products to exchange.

From the Teyas: Containers of dried buffalo meat. Tanned buffalo hides, some with the hair left on for warm sleeping robes, some scraped clean for tough, flexible leather. Buffalo bones worked into tools, horns carved into spoons and ladles. Long tough sinews for sewing and bow strings. Tallow and fat for flavoring stews, for soothing injuries and for protecting skin from harsh weather. Sturdy moccasins decorated with colored porcupine quills, and long, fringed deerskin shirts for cold days. Fine stone for tools, and shells from far away for ornaments. Red stone pipes and strong tobacco to go with them. And captives, always captives, raided from other tribes to help with the never-ending labor of each community.

From the pueblos: Corn on the ears, as dried kernels or ground into meal. Multicolored beans and dried squash. Piñon nuts, local tobacco, medicinal herbs from the mountains. Pottery of varying sizes and shapes, some for plain cooking, some decorated for storing things. Cotton blankets, clothing, headbands. Turkey feathers woven into light, warm robes, and colorful feathers from tropical birds traded from the south. Beads of many sizes, shapes and materials strung into necklaces and pendants. Chipped stone points, large ones for spears, smaller ones for arrows, tiny ones for bird-darts, slender ones for grinding holes. Flint knives and scrapers. Gambling pieces, toys, bird-bone flutes, copper bells, clay whistles. And so much more.

Many things changed hands. The bargaining went on all day. Hopping Bird, Toba and others who spoke several languages were kept busy running from one situation to another.

One group of strangers who came to the trading had traveled from far to the south. They were Toba's Aztec people. He welcomed them extravagantly, then disappeared with them into a kiva to meet with the elders. Flame assumed they brought news of the Shining Ones who had visited Cicuye when she was a small child. Though the older people talked about them with awe and humor, they worried what would happen if they returned. Flame herself didn't remember much about them. Just that there was a lot of confusion, of coming and going. The strangers had pale faces and hairy chins, and shiny, hard skin they could take off. They brought many people from the south to do the hard work and some strange animals they ate. Huge beasts that frightened her carried the Shining Ones on their backs. They had big teeth, and she was convinced they ate children. When one of the Shining Ones scooped her up and set her on top of one of these creatures, she screamed in terror.

～

One of the strangers had stayed behind when the others went away. This one didn't shine. He was an old man who wore a long blue robe. The elders gave him a room in the pueblo and some of the women brought him food every day. Toba, whom he called "*Cristóbal,*" was the young slave who helped him, a brown-skinned youth from the south who had learned the talk of the Shining Ones and quickly picked up the Cicuye language.

Flame and the other children laughed when the old man tried to talk with them. The Cicuye words they tried to teach him sounded funny when they came out of his mouth. They ran around laughing with their fingers crossed, the forefinger over the thumb in the way he had showed them, shouting "*Ave María*" and "*Pax Cristi*" until the elders made them stop.

The Shining Ones had left with the old man some strange animals, bigger than dogs with thick, curly hair. They ate grass. The old man tried to teach some of the Cicuye boys to look after these animals, but the boys forgot and the coyotes ate them. The wooly skin of one of them was saved, and the old man slept on it.

When the old man died after several seasons at Cicuye, Cristóbal (Toba) stayed at the pueblo, moved in with the family of the girl he loved and made himself useful in many ways. He learned the languages of all the people who came to trade. He visited their villages in turn, learned their customs and met their leaders. He listened to their news and gossip and was particularly important in times of trade, travel or tension. And of course, he was also a fund of knowledge about the ways of the Shining Ones and of the life he had left behind. Now Toba slept on the wooly animal skin.

⌒

One afternoon, Flame went with Mother and Broken Wing down to the Teya camp to trade. They lugged some of Mother's pots and jars, one filled with dried beans, another with corn meal. When Flame tried to make pots, they still turned out lopsided. But from the clay, she created little animals that made people laugh and whistles that chirped like the birds they resembled. She carried some of them in one of Mother's painted pots.

Walking among the tipis, dodging dogs and children, greeting some of the women they had talked with earlier, they encountered the man Flame privately called "Bear Claws" for the necklace around his neck. She didn't know his real name, but he was obviously important among the Teyas. She had seen him several times. He always laughed at her, probably remembering how she had fallen at his feet. She tried to avoid him: he seemed so big, so powerful, so foreign, that she was somewhat afraid of him. Now she saw with dismay that Mother was heading for the tipi where he lived with his women and children.

She saw something else, too. Shining white against his chest hung the big bone bead! The one handed down through the ancestors! Surely Bead Maker wouldn't have traded it away, something as important as that! Where was Bead Maker? Where was Grandfather? What should she do? She noticed that the thong holding the bead was new and remembered that the one Bead Maker was using was frayed and worn. Perhaps Bear Claws had found it fallen on the ground. How could she get it back? Mother and Broken Wing were going on ahead.

⟃

Clutching the pot against her chest, pretending to be braver than she felt, Flame walked up to face Bear Claws. She looked at him more boldly than she knew was respectful for pueblo girls with their elders. She pointed to the bone bead and indicating with signs and talking slowly and clearly in her own language, told him that the bone pendant belonged to her people and he should give it back.

The big man looked down at her, laughed, and invited her to sit down and discuss the situation. "What do you have to trade?" he signed. Flame thrust Mother's pot towards him, showed him one of the little animals, and blew on one of the bird whistles. Interested, the man set the pot on his knee and took out the little animals one by one. A bear, a dog with a stubby tail, a squirrel with a piñon nut in its paws, a rabbit with floppy ears, a fox with a pointed nose and bushy tail, and a strange-looking buffalo—Flame had never seen a live one—that started him laughing all over again. He tried all the whistles, which brought nearby children and dogs to see what was happening.

By this time, Mother had come back, and seeing the situation sent Broken Wing to find Grandfather. When the Teya saw that Mother, too, wanted the bone bead returned, that somehow it was important, he signed "No trade," spoke a while in his own language for the benefit of his approaching friends, got up an started to walk away.

Grandfather arrived, followed by Hopping Bird. Their talk with Bear Claws became animated, heated, angry. His friends came closer, looking fierce. Finally, Grandfather turned to Mother and Flame and reported, "He drives a hard bargain. He found the bone on the ground. He likes it and wants to keep it. He'll only trade in exchange for—Flame! We'll have to be careful. This could get touchy."

Flame's heart sank. Wasn't she worth more than the old bone, even though it came from the ancestors? The Teya was looking at her now in a way that made her very nervous. He grabbed her arm and looked fierce as he pushed her back down on the ground.

"Wait here. Don't move," commanded Grandfather. He went off

with Hopping Bird toward the pueblo. Mother and Broken Wing went back to the tipi to trade and visit with the women. Bear Claws moved away to talk with some other men. Every now and then they all looked at her and laughed.

Flame sat there alone, frightened, wondering if she would be taken away to follow the buffalo. Would Bear Claws use her as one of his women? Would she be a slave, carrying loads and scraping skins until she wore out? Would they treat her kindly, or not? What would it be like to eat fresh buffalo meat, roasted over the coals, dripping with grease and fat? How would she survive times of hunger when the buffalo could not be found and the dried meat had all been eaten? How much would she miss the corn, beans and squash, and the storerooms full of the plentiful harvests of the pueblo? Without the daily hours spent grinding corn, how would she use her time? Butchering the buffalo carcasses, drying the meat, tanning the skins and shaping them into bags and clothes? Moving camp from one place to another and struggling with tipis and dogs?

She watched the people moving back and forth, wondering what they were like. She studied the painted designs on nearby tipis, wondering if she could get used to living in one. She laughed as she watched a small child staggering in pursuit of a puppy, and then fought tears because he reminded her of Baby Brother whom she might never see again. Except for a few curious looks, everybody ignored her. She wondered if Mother was watching, but she couldn't see where she had gone.

A young boy wandered over and sat down near her. He looked thin, tired, hungry, anxious. Flame realized he was a captive. He reminded her a little of Hopping Bird. She wondered if Hopping Bird had looked little and scared like this boy.

⌒

She had often heard Hopping Bird's story. Snatched from his people by raiders, he had been traded from tribe to tribe for several years, picking up languages, customs and skills along the way. Then, traveling with the Teyas, staggering under a huge load, he had tripped in a hole, breaking his leg. While the warriors debated whether to leave him behind to fend for himself and get eaten by wolves or to kill him first, for he was no use to them now, a woman who had treated him kindly rearranged the drag poles behind two big dogs and helped him into the carrier between them. With his leg wrapped in rawhide, he bounced and bumped painfully across the distances until they came to Cicuye. Here he was traded for a pot of beans, and "Pot of Beans" was what he was called for many months. He was half starved, sick in body and spirit. Grandmother's family took him in and tended him until he decided to live and began to mend. His leg finally healed, but crooked. He walked with a heavy limp, throwing out his arms for balance, and people began referring to him as the hopping bird he resembled.

At first they gave him easy work: sorting beans, twining fibers into cord, repairing sandals and baskets. As he got stronger, he began kneading clay, scraping hides, weaving rush mats. He learned the language quickly. Though he couldn't walk far, his hands were strong and skillful. He spun cotton fibers into thread for weaving, helped with the tedious job of grinding, piercing and polishing bits of shell and turquoise for ornaments. He chipped stone into arrow points, knives and scrapers. He could work with animal skins, turning them into sturdy moccasins, fringed shirts, or decorated bags the way he had learned from the plains people. He was funny, his jokes and humorous observations of individuals and events kept people laughing. With his knowledge of the languages and customs of the many tribes and what he learned from visitors from other places, he became a valuable interpreter.

Though he was still considered an outsider, he had earned the respect and affection of many of the Cicuye folks. Now he had moved in with Broken Wing. Flame hoped they would soon have children to cheer their loneliness.

~

Lonely. Flame herself felt lonely, sitting there wondering about her future. She had always heard that the Teyas were unpredictable, and that they stole children. If they stole her away and she never saw her family, friends, pueblo or valley again, she would be very lonely indeed.

She looked back at the little boy. How lonely he must be! There was something endearing about him as he chewed on a piece of dried buffalo meat and shoved away a dog that wanted a bite. He might make a good little brother, she thought. Or maybe a son for Broken Wing and Hopping Bird. Maybe he could help the two crippled birds to fly again.

She started to move over to sit beside him, but a glare and a gesture from Bear Claws stopped her. The little boy noticed and offered her a piece of the meat in his hand. But by now, Flame was too scared to want to eat anything at all. Everything around her—tipis, people, dogs, even children—seemed threatening and hostile. Her stomach knotted up and she began to shake.

At last, she saw Grandfather and Hopping Bird returning. Grandfather was carrying a fine turkey feather robe and a cotton blanket painted with designs of corn plants and rain clouds. Hopping Bird carried a splendid necklace with a large turquoise pendant surrounded by shell beads that came from the big waters to the west.

Bear Claws and his friends strode over to meet them. For a long while, they talked and argued while other people gathered around to see what was happening. Voices got loud and angry. Flame was terrified. She noticed Mother and Broken Wing watching anxiously. Some Cicuye warriors were coming near because some Teyas were reaching for their weapons. Would there be a big fight? With her in the middle?

At last, the men sat down on the ground, brought out pipes and began to smoke. The tension was broken. The talk sounded more friendly. The warriors wandered away and everybody relaxed.

Bear Claws accepted the feather robe and the cotton blanket, handing them to one of his women to put inside the tipi. He put the necklace on over his head, where it hung next to the bear claws. He stood up, walked over to Flame and pulled her to her feet. He slipped the thong holding the bone bead over her head and gave her a shove toward her grandfather. Flame was ready to cry with relief—but then she saw that she had forgotten something.

Her mother's pot with the little animals inside was still there where she had been sitting. She went back to fetch it, but Bear Claws grabbed it first. No longer afraid, she demanded it back. Bear Claws scowled, and Flame shouted the first Teya word she had learned. "Trade, trade!" she demanded. Bear Claws' eyebrows went up, questioning. Flame pointed to the little boy. Once again, Bear Claws started to laugh, reached back to grab the boy's arm, and shoved him toward Flame. He walked off with the pot under one arm, blowing on one of the little whistles. Everybody started laughing.

⌒

The boy and Flame stared at each other in astonishment. What had happened?

Hopping Bird bent down to speak to the boy. When he looked up, his face was shining and tears spilled from his eyes. "This boy is from my people," Hopping Bird said quietly. "I used to know his mother. If the Teyas know we care about him, they may try to take him back."

The little group walked up the slope toward the shelter of their stone pueblo on the ridge, which for Flame, especially now, was a warm and comforting home. Mother carried the well-tanned buffalo robe and the large ladle carved from buffalo horn, while Broken Wing carried two pairs of sturdy moccasins and a gourd full of rich buffalo fat they had gotten in trade. Hopping Bird followed the boy closely and protectively.

Grandfather brought up the rear, looking very tired. When Flame offered him the bone bead, he smiled, touched it and said, "You can wear it now. You've earned it. I know you will look after it carefully. I'll shorten the thong so it will hang next to your heart instead of your belly button." He put his arm around her shoulders for help in climbing the slope, or out of affection for his granddaughter. Flame wasn't sure. It didn't matter.

⌒

The next day when Flame went up to the rooftop, she was astonished to see that the Teyas had gone. No tipis, no dogs, no people, no campfires, no Bear Claws. Just a string of little black dots moving down the valley, disappearing into the distance.

The harvest waited.

5

"Cristo is Here" (1625 AD)

LITTLE DOVE ENTERED the large mission kitchen with delight. All the familiar bustle of people at work, the good smells of cooking stew, the slap-slapping of hands shaping tortillas, the coming and going of the workers, the skittering of chickens pecking at spilled grains of corn or wheat. She carefully emptied the corn meal from the pot she carried into a large container by the door. She and her mother had ground it this morning. It was their day to share.

The Pecos women doing the cooking that day were cheerful, trading jokes and gossip while they chopped meat and vegetables for the stew simmering in the huge copper kettle and stirred the beans and chile heating in large clay pots. They worked at a long wooden table and the raised stone-and-clay stove that were easier on their joints than the floor-level *metates* and fireplaces they used at home. A couple of them were using steel knives that were mostly worn out from much sharpening. Others sliced and chopped with sharp obsidian blades selected from a basket of stone tools. Gourds, baskets, and clay jars of various sizes and shapes held herbs and spices, dried meat, peaches and assorted vegetables. Strings of onions, garlic and chile peppers hung from pegs in the rafters.

Fat Marta/Big Ears, one of her mother's sisters, threw one arm about Little Dove's neck in a big hug, while with the other she waved the wooden spoon she had been using to stir the stew.

"So you like it here, Little Dove! You come in every day to see what's happening, even when you don't have to. Are you looking for a handsome soldier or a mule driver among the people we feed here? Or maybe it's the *fiscal,* Ramón, who grabs your fancy?

Little Dove was used to such teasing. She slithered away from the embrace. Skinny Benita/Blue Shell handed her a tortilla wrapped around a spoonful of beans. "Try this and tell me if it tastes good," she invited. She did, and yes, it tasted very good.

Pancho/Turtle was unloading firewood from two donkeys just outside the doorway. Juanita/Yellow Melon brought in some steaming loaves of wheat bread from the round-topped outdoor oven. María/ Four Fingers was plucking a fresh-killed chicken. José/Eagle Feather was setting up long plank tables and benches where people could sit and eat. Everybody who worked at the mission had two names. The kitchen fed a lot of people every day after the midday mass: the workers for the day, visitors and some of the Pecos people who needed extra food or help.

Marta/Big Ears waved her wooden spoon toward a group of sad-looking people sitting on the ground in the sunshine outside the doorway. "They came in last night," she told Little Dove very quietly. "They have left their pueblo, their relatives, everything they cared about. The Spaniards were treating them badly and demanding too much tribute. The priest was destroying their sacred objects and whipping those who didn't go to mass. They were starving and had no choice. Maybe they'll stay here where life is better, or maybe they'll join the Apaches on the buffalo plains. It's so hard for them . . . "

A crisis interrupted her. A rooster had flown up on the stove and burned its feet. He was flapping around frantically, squawking in distress, until someone shooed him outside. Everybody laughed and made jokes about it. Little Dove laughed until her sides ached, even though she felt sorry for the rooster. Marta/Big Ears wiped away a tear and commented, "Maybe there's some sort of lesson here for all of us."

⌒

Carrying her empty pot, Little Dove wandered through the *convento,* the working area of the mission, looking at all the familiar scenes. There were many rooms, some large, some small, many ranged around small courtyards or with entryways to the outside. Storage rooms held tools and harnesses, farm implements and an anvil. In other rooms, baskets of wool and piles of hides and tanned leather were stacked along with finished blankets of wool, cotton and soft deerskin. Corn, beans and other farm products were waiting to be shared as needed. Closer to the church were supplies for the many religious ceremonies. Upstairs on the second level were the rooms where Father Andrés lived and worked and where visitors sometimes stayed. There were small rooms for his two *fiscales,* Christian Indian helpers, who had come with him from far to the south; and there was one for the rotating doorkeepers who greeted guests in the large area beside the stairs. A horse and two mules watched Little Dove curiously from the sheltered corral outside a doorway. When she reached out to pat the horse, it snickered and shied away. Little Dove laughed.

She passed the carpentry shop where her father was carving designs in a piece of wood with chisel and mallet. He saw her and tossed his head in greeting. Little Dove knew how he liked to work with wood and the metal tools the Spaniards had brought and taught him how to use. He had become a skilled carpenter and had been sent for a month all the way to Santa Fe to work on the new *Casas Reales*, the government buildings. He worked happily here in the carpentry shop whenever his fields or the religious life of the pueblo did not need his attention. He liked many of the things the mission had brought, but had not become a Christian.

In another room, Luis, a tall, lean *fiscal,* was teaching several boys to sing a psalm for the next feast day. "*Exaltabote, Domine,*" their voices rang out. The language was neither Spanish nor Pecos, but Little Dove remembered that the words meant, "I shall praise you, oh Lord." She listened with pleasure to the singing and imagined how fine it would sound later in the big church.

In another room, two women and an older man were weaving, turning wool from sheep's backs into soft, warm cloth. In still another room, four Apache women from the buffalo plains were working soft deerskins and tough buffalo hide into moccasins for the coming cold weather. Father Andrés always said, "Full bellies and warm feet make working here a special treat." But Little Dove giggled at the thought, for Father Andrés had a very skinny belly and always wore barefoot sandals, even in the coldest weather. Another woman was making simple tunics from tanned deerskins, which were warmer and quicker to make than the traditional cotton *mantas* the pueblo women usually wore. Little Dove was wearing one of these tunics. It slipped over her head and was belted around her waist with a red woven cotton sash, with fringes dangling from the hem and the sleeves. She had stitched a turquoise bead on the front for decoration. The women were chattering away in their own language while they worked.

Nearby, a group of children were learning Spanish. "*Uno, dos, tres, toca la campana, cuatro, cinco seis, me gusta la mañana . . .*" Little Dove sang along with them, "One two three, the bell is ringing, four, five, six, I like the morning." She had learned the song long ago.

Past the workrooms, four young men were waiting for whatever errands they might be sent on. When Little Dove peered at them, they quickly concealed the gaming pieces they had been using for a gambling game. Father Andrés would not approve.

Out beyond were the enclosures where the sheep and goats were brought in for safety or for shearing. A team of men were laying up heavy adobe bricks for the wall of a new room, while a gang of women smoothed the edges and sides with mud plaster. The Pecos people had built their pueblo with rocks held together with adobe mud. But Father Andrés and his helpers had shown them how to mold and use the bricks, which were sturdy and convenient—and a lot of work. Little Dove had helped plaster many of the walls in the *convento* and church, both inside and out. She felt pleased to be able to help, especially whenever she looked at the areas where she had worked. One of the women called to her to come and help, but Little Dove went on her way.

⌒

Outside the *convento*, she looked up at the towering walls of the Great Church. It was almost finished, and much of it already had been whitewashed. The six stubby towers rose above the roof. Most of the scaffolding had been taken down, though some workers were still putting finishing touches on one of the towers. The heavy wooden doors with shiny metal handles had designs carved in them that had been chiseled by Father.

Little Dove was always awestruck by the church. It was a splendid, huge enclosure soaring up to the sky. Father Andrés spoke often about how proud the Pecos people should be that they were able to work together to create such a wonderful home for *Cristo* and his *santos*. This was the biggest and the best church in all these northern provinces of the Spanish empire. Little Dove didn't know what he meant by that, but it sounded impressive. All of the people in the pueblo could fit inside when called together for mass, particularly on feast days. The men stood or knelt on one side, the women and children on the other. Light streamed in through the high windows, and the slanted one on the roof lit up the altar. The shining cross carried in procession by boys in white robes and bearing colored banners began and ended the ceremonies. Sweet-smelling incense smoke swirled toward the roof. The many candles made pinpoints of light. Colored painting on hides attached to the walls represented angels with circles of light around their heads and improbable wings attached to their shoulders. The picture of the beautiful lady, Our Lady of the Angels, looked down from her place over the altar: she had come all the way from Spain a long time ago. The mysterious sacred meal of God's flesh honored the dead man hanging from the cross with blood dripping down his side. The choirboys sang the psalms, while the *fiscales* led the prayers, read wonderful stories from the sacred book, and translated Father Andrés' words. Though Father Andrés spoke the Pecos language, sort of, his pronunciation was usually so strange that people would laugh instead of listen, so he used translators on formal occasions. There was much to delight the eye and ear, but Little Dove didn't really understand much of what it all meant. It was all very dramatic and confusing. The inside of the church was always cold, and she was often shivering when she came out into the sunshine.

Prayer feathers decorated the huge cross erected outside the church door. She wondered who had put them there.

⌒

"Hola, Palomita!" She turned and saw the *fiscal* Ramón smiling at her. "You don't work today?" Ramón was as round and cheerful as Luis was lean and stern. He told wonderful stories about *Cristo* and his *santos* in easy ways people could understand. One of them had all the little boys practicing with their slings to bring down the evil giant. He painted some of the pictures on the hides hanging inside the church and taught others to do so, too. He spoke to her, as usual, in Spanish.

"I'm NOT Palomita!" the girl retorted. "My name is Little Dove, for the little white birds that pop up unexpectedly from the bushes."

"Of course," replied Ramón. "That's what Palomita means. It's the symbol of the Holy Spirit, which also pops up unexpectedly out of the bushes. Watch out for it, Palomita, Little Dove. It may surprise you."

They both laughed because this same conversation had been repeated many times. Little Dove liked Ramón, but he always left her feeling confused. They stood together in silence for a minute.

"That's quite a sight!" Ramón marveled, gesturing with his chin toward the great Pecos Pueblo nearby. Little Dove followed his gaze, taking in the huge buildings just beyond the boundary wall separating the mission area from the pueblo. Three and sometimes four stories high, terraces at each level formed the roof of the apartments below. The whitewash coating on most of the walls shone in the sunshine. She could hear the murmur of many voices, the shrill cries of children, the soft crunching of many hand stones grinding the daily corn on the *metates,* the snapping sound of someone breaking sticks for a cooking fire. From somewhere over there, a rooster crowed and a dog barked. The voice of the watcher on the high place shouted teasing jokes at some hunters bringing in a fresh-killed deer and then greeted a messenger from another pueblo. A drum thumped softly to the sound of a flute. She could see people moving about and working on the terraces outside their doorways. Other people were coming and going back and forth from their cornfields, to the creek or to tend the mission fields. A donkey brayed, and she heard people laughing. It was a busy, lively scene that she liked to see and be part of.

Ramón started to leave, then turned back to Little Dove. "Did you see the latest group of refugees in the kitchen?" he asked her. "Father Andrés is furious at the way they have been treated. He is writing angry letters to the governor and to the *custos* head of the missions. There are strict laws about proper respect and care for the native people by the *gachupines.* (He used an Aztec work for the Spaniards, "the men who wear spurs.") But too many ignore those laws. The poor people have been robbed of so much . . ."

Little Dove stumbled around wondering what to say. "The boys will be happy to carry the letters," she stammered. "They like the chance to ride the mission mules." That wasn't really what she wanted to say, so she started again. "How can some of those *gachupines* be so bad to us while others treat us fairly?"

Ramón studied the pebbles on the ground. "The Spaniards are like people everywhere," he finally said. "Just like the rest of us, some are good and some are bad and most of them, like us, are somewhere in between." He pushed groups of pebbles into separate piles with his foot. "We just have to figure out who are the ones we can work with and to do the best we can with whatever comes along."

"Ramón, why did you become a *fiscal*, helping the missions with Father Andrés?" As she spoke, Little Dove knew that it was not proper for a young girl to ask such a direct question to an older person, but she wanted to know.

Ramón was not offended. With a faraway look in his eyes, he explained, "The Spanish soldiers came to my little village far away to the south. They took my father and many of the other men away with chains on their legs. We never knew what happened to them. My mother and I were sent to a big ranch where my mother was put to work in the kitchen. I was quite small, and eventually they sent me to be raised in the nearby mission. The *padres* treated me kindly, taught me many things, and became the only family I knew. As I got older and went on errands around the countryside, I could see how they were trying to help my people who were often abused by the soldiers and the ranchers. When they asked me to come here to help Father Andrés, I thought maybe in this way I could help other people. So, here I am!"

⌒

They heard a shout and saw someone running up the trail toward them. It was Wolf Tail, Little Dove's older brother who now wanted to be called Pablo.

"It's here! The wagon! The BELL!" he shouted, and dashed into the *convento* to find Father Andrés.

Sure enough, soon a small procession came into sight. Six soldiers with shining helmets and breastplates, the sun glinting on the steel tips of their lances, rode in front on tired-looking horses. After them came a large four-wheeled wagon with canvas stretched over the top, pulled by a team of eight mules. Bells jingled on their harness, little flags fluttered from the poles at the corners of the wagon. The driver, a handsome-looking fellow with a little black mustache and colored ribbons on his hat, gave Little Dove a big wink as he brought the team neatly to a stop in front of the church. Behind the wagon straggled a group of militia, Spanish settlers and pueblo Indians, riding on an assortment of mules and a donkey. They wore broad-brimmed hats and padded leather jackets. They carried shields made of buffalo hide, bows and arrows and spears with stone-tipped points. Leading the procession along with the *capitán* of the soldiers was a Franciscan priest, his blue robe hitched up around his knees. He looked tired and disagreeable. Little Dove suspected his butt hurt as well as his feet. It was a long way from the Mexico City.

Father Andrés came rushing out of the doorway, his tattered blue robe swirling around his feet.

"In the name of God and the people of Pecos Pueblo, we welcome you," he cried. The soldiers dismounted and stretched their weary bodies while the mission boys of the day unhitched the mules and led them and the horses to the corral for water and fodder.

"Rest yourselves, friends," Father Andrés invited the newcomers. "There's food in the kitchen and shade where you can relax." Turning to the people gathered around, he advised them, "The supply wagons reach us only once every three years. We will give thanks to God at the midday mass. Then we will eat a bit and rest before uncovering the wagon to see what has been sent to us. Go now, back to your tasks. We'll gather for mass a little later."

The *capitán* and the priest accompanied him inside. There were formal papers to sign and much news to share. The journey from Mexico City had taken the caravan with supplies for all the northern missions six months. No wonder the priest's butt hurt!

⌒

"Hey, Palomita! At last our bell is here!" Her brother Wolf Tail was smiling down at her. He looked so delighted that she smiled back.

"Wolf Tail, why do you talk to me in Spanish?" she asked him in the Pecos language.

"I'm, Pablo now," he responded in Spanish. "We all have to speak Spanish. Even you."

"I thought you were up on the mesa with Miguel and the sheep. What are you doing down here?"

"I came down on an errand and will stay awhile. Miguel has other helpers. He teaches us so much about the sheep and the goats. We're learning how to care for them, how to keep them fed and safe from the wolves and the bears, how to shear the wool and to kill and eat them when necessary. He tells such wonderful stories of his home in far-off Spain, about the huge ocean he crossed in a ship with sails that moved with the wind, about the many things he saw in the land of the Aztecs and about the long journey across the deserts to get here. When he goes back to the ranch where he works we'll be able to tend the sheep and the goats by ourselves."

"Do you know how to hunt? Can you make stone arrow points? Can you trap deer and other animals with nets and snares? Can you tend the cornfields so that the harvest is plentiful? Do you know our sacred dances that connect us with the ancestors?"

"Nah! Why should I? I'm a mission boy now. I can help with the mass and sing the psalms and read the Bible lessons and lead the prayers. '*Pater noster, qui en caelo est.*' See? 'Our Father, who is in heaven . . .' Don't you know that one yet? Father Andrés tells me if I work hard and learn more, he'll make me a *fiscal*! That would be great! Unless I decide to become a soldier with a shining helmet and a fine horse and a gun that spits fire and kills our enemies."

"Which enemies do you have in mind?" Little Dove was laughing at his shifting enthusiasms.

"Who knows? There will be some. But now, the bell has arrived, and its sound will proclaim to all the countryside that *Cristo* is here!"

⌣

Little Dove wandered back to the pueblo carrying her empty pot, her mind swirling. So many changes were happening. It was very confusing. Grandmother was on the terrace outside her doorway grinding some herbs in a small stone bowl.

"What took you so long, Little Dove? Were you watching the supply wagon and flirting with the soldiers?"

"No, Grandmother. The bell has come. But tell me, please, what was it like here before the Spaniards came?"

Grandmother's expression changed. She jerked her chin in the direction of the church and spat with contempt.

"Before the *gachupines* came, we were a free, independent, proud, rich pueblo. We were the Cicuye people then. Our traders roamed far and wide, our warriors were feared, our storerooms were full, our elders were respected, our dances and ceremonies full of energy, the Ancient Ones smiled on us, we lived in harmony with the spirits of the sky and of the earth . . .

"Now they call us the Pecos. The *gachupines* rule us. They send their wagons to empty our storerooms. They take away our people to work in their fields and houses. They steal our youngsters and upset the harmony."

"But not all the Spaniards are bad." Little Dove was reflecting what Ramón had said. "They have brought us many new things and taught us to raise new crops and to look after animals we didn't have before. And Father Andrés tries so hard to protect us from the *gachupines*."

"Yes, Father Andrés is a good man," Grandmother admitted. "But that's what makes him so dangerous. We can't hate him. Look what he's doing to us.

"He's luring away our young people so they forget the wisdom of the ancestors. He wastes our time in building that huge house for *Cristo*. We work for the mission instead of for ourselves and our people. He is destroying respect for our elders, condemning our gods and our whole way of life. True, he treats us kindly and with respect—most of the time. He doesn't interfere much with our dances and ceremonies. He tries to speak with us in our own language. But he will leave and others will come, like the ones the refugees who arrived last night were escaping from, priests who enter the kivas and destroy the *kachinas* and whip the people who don't go to mass. That priest who was here before Father Andrés was like that, and we hear of others at other pueblos."

Her eyes were flashing as she pounded the grinding stone furiously. Little Dove had never seen her so angry and felt alarmed. Grandmother usually was calm and kind to everybody.

After a minute she continued more quietly, "These poor settlers who come from so far away, I feel sorry for them. They don't know how to live here, they're helpless. They need our corn to feed themselves and our hunters to bring them meat and deerskins, and our potters to make their bowls and pots, and our basket makers to make containers and mats and our flintknappers to provide knives and arrow points when their metal ones wear out, and our people to gather piñon nuts in the fall and our weavers to make the cotton blankets they trade. Look at Miguel the shepherd. He's a nice enough lad, knows about sheep and not much else. Wolf Tail has asked me to prepare herbs for Miguel's toothache, which any good pueblo man would be able to gather for himself."

⌒

The midday mass was a joyous occasion. The light from the windows, the sparkling of the beeswax candles, the shining cross, the vessels on the altar, the colors of the robes and the banners, the painted pictures on the walls, all seemed to glow more brightly than usual. The voices of Father Andrés and the *fiscales* rang out with enthusiasm, and the people's responses were loud and energetic. "*Gratias deo*," they shouted, "*Jubilate!*" Thanks be to God! Rejoice! The picture of our Lady of the Angels smiled down from its place above the altar. Wolf Tail/Pablo carried the cross in the procession. Little Dove knew that this was a special honor and felt glad for him.

Later Little Dove, her mother and father joined the crowd to watch the unloading of the wagon. Wolf Tail helped carry the things as they were unloaded into the *convento*.

When the canvas cover was removed, wonders emerged. As the *fiscales* opened bags, boxes and bales, they held up the contents for all to see. Two big new copper kettles for the kitchen, each filled with small bags of seeds and spices. Metal tools of all sorts, some with wooden handles attached, and some with just the iron and steel parts for which the local carpenters could attach handles themselves. Farming tools: hoes, shovels, sickles. Carpentry tools: axes, saws, chisels, hammers, big and little nails and spikes, hinges and door handles. Tools for the kitchen: knives, spoons, cleavers, ladles, pots and pans. There were bales of cloth of shining white and various colors, sturdy canvas and loose sacking, fine silks for church vestments. New steel needles, big and little, and skeins of bright thread for sewing or embroidery. A new blue robe for Father Andrés: the people murmured approval because his old one was so ragged and worn out. Boxes of fine beeswax candles to use on feast days instead of the usual tallow ones that smoked and sputtered erratically. Paper and ink for writing. A new prayer book and one of hymns and psalms to sing. Jugs of communion wine. Boxes of the dark Mexican chocolate that made such a pleasant drink and cones of brown sugar to sweeten it. A box of small shiny crosses to hang around the necks of the faithful as special gifts and small images of different *santos*.

With great excitement, Luis brought out a small pump organ and sat it on the ground. He showed Wolf Tail how to pump the bellows, and his fingers danced over the keys, a rapt expression on his face. The sound was unfamiliar, but suddenly Little Dove recognized one of the tunes sung in church and she hopped up and down with delight. From more boxes emerged two fiddles and a guitar. The Pecos had heard Spanish settlers playing them and were eager to learn. The music would add to the choir voices and enrich the mass, to the envy of all their neighbors. And carefully packed were some large bowls of thin, white ceramic with blue designs painted on them. Father Andrés explained that they had come from China, a huge country far away across the western ocean, but that didn't mean much to the gathered people.

There were many more marvelous things. At last they came to the BELL. Father and Ramón carefully pried open its crate and hefted it on top so all could see. It gleamed tan and golden in the sunshine. A strong hoop was cast into the top to hang it by. The round clapper that would ring it hung just below the broad open bottom. Letters and designs roughened the surface of the metal. Ramón tapped it with a little stick. The only sound it made was a small, dull "ping." The people groaned with disappointment. "Not to worry," Father Andrés assured them. "When it's hanging in its honored place in the tower, its tongue will be free and it will sing out loud and clear. We'll put it there tomorrow, but for now we'll leave it here where everyone can look at it and touch it."

Little Dove walked over for a closer look. She ran her fingers over the cold metal, tried to read the raised letters, but wasn't sure what they said, and she "pinged" the edge with the little stick. She wondered why Wolf Tail thought this bell would proclaim to the world that *Cristo* was here. It seemed very unlikely to her. Why all the great fuss about it?

The next day Little Dove was working in the kitchen plucking chicken and listening to an argument among the cooks about whether the new steel knives were really any better than the traditional obsidian ones.

Somebody outside shouted, "*CIBOLEROS COMING!*" She knew that the *ciboleros* were Spanish settlers with pueblo helpers who went out to the plains country to hunt buffalo, returning with carts full of dried buffalo meat, hides, useful bones and other buffalo products.

She peered out the door and saw six two-wheeled carts, *carretas,* each pulled by two oxen, approaching the mission. The drivers, hunters, butchers and hide-scrapers were walking beside them protected by six soldiers on horseback. She knew they would be hungry and would stop for a while for food and rest. Everybody would welcome the dried meat they brought.

Suddenly she heard a scream, followed by more, and a great wailing. The plains Apache women working at the mission started howling. The pueblo women joined them. Little Dove looked more closely. A number of people were tied to the *carretas*, men, women and children, dragging along among the walkers. Captives, she realized, taken as Spanish slaves.

"Our people!" cried the Apache women. "Our allies, our friends, our trading partners!" cried the pueblo women.

As the procession drew up in front of the mission, Father Andrés dashed out. Little Dove could see him furiously arguing with the soldiers and leaders of the *ciboleros*. Taking slaves was forbidden by Spanish Colonial Law. The *fiscales* joined him, as did several of the Pecos elders. People were shouting and shaking their fists. One soldier thrust his spear against Father Andrés' chest. The Pecos elders pulled him away.

Finally, a compromise was reached. The children would be rescued and brought to Pecos to live. The adults would have to go on to captivity. "Governor's orders," insisted the *capitán* of the soldiers.

"Illegal nonsense!" replied Father Andrés.

"We will care for them," promised the Pecos elders.

"I shall protest to the authorities," declared Father Andrés.

Some of the *ciboleros* looked unhappy because their objections had been overruled by the soldiers. The mission would feed the captives, but not the soldiers nor the hard-working *ciboleros*.

Father Andrés was crying as he and the *fiscales* carried the small children into the *convento*. The Apache women were crying as they brought new moccasins for the bleeding feet of the captives. The pueblo women were crying as they carried pots of stew and beans and baskets of tortillas to the captives. The captives were crying as they watched their children disappear through the doorway. The children were crying because they were being separated from their parents and because everybody else was crying. Even some of the *ciboleros* were crying because they had felt so helpless to change the situation.

Little Dove was crying too. Why were there some such terrible scenes among the happy ones that surrounded her? The sounds of wailing and lamentations continued long after the procession disappeared along the trail to Santa Fe.

❧

Later, Little Dove watched her father and some other men trying to wrestle the heavy bell up the narrow stairway to the bell tower. It wasn't easy, and they were having a hard time.

She went on home feeling sad, angry and confused. Why were the *gachupines* so cruel? Taking captives as slaves was a common practice everywhere, she knew. Some of them lived at the pueblo. Life was often difficult and workers of all kinds were needed. Sometimes they were treated kindly, taught many skills and eventually set free. Sometimes they were treated badly, beaten and overworked until they died. And sometimes the men captured were sent off to the mines farther south where their lives were brutal and short.

She had never seen the painful separation of families before. The cries echoed in her ears. The bleeding feet of the captives, the spears of the soldiers, the helpless passivity of the *ciboleros* and the fury of Father Andrés replayed themselves in her mind.

But not all the Spaniards were cruel! Many were kindhearted and hard working, sharing what they knew with the Pecos people and learning from them how to live in this high, cold country. They were far from home and often lonely.

She thought of Miguel the shepherd, of the handsome mule driver, and of the carpenter who had taught Father his craft. She thought of the farmers who had showed the Pecos how to plant wheat and turn it into bread in the round-topped adobe ovens. Others had helped them plant trees that produced the juicy peaches and red apples everybody liked so much. She remembered the kind woman who saved the life of one of her cousins during a difficult childbirth and who still came to visit the mother and healthy child.

The Spaniards had also learned from the Pecos people about planting small corn patches at different times so that an early frost would not wipe out the whole crop. They had come to appreciate beautifully tanned deerskins, the usefulness of stone tools and the yearlong value of piñon nuts collected in the fall. They depended on the skills of the pueblo potters and weavers for many things they needed.

Most often they traded with the Pecos instead of simply taking what they wanted. True, some of them took women by force. Others cherished and married pueblo women and cared for them and their children. As Ramón had said, some are bad, some are good, and most of us are somewhere in between.

Father Andrés was special, even though Grandmother had called him dangerous. He had presented her with one of the shiny little crosses that had come with the wagon, personally slipping its thong over her head with a blessing. It gleamed beside the turquoise bead on her tunic.

⌒

On her way down to the creek on an errand for her mother, she met Grandfather returning to the pueblo. His usual smile of greeting suddenly turned to rage. He ripped the cross from her neck, snapping the cord. He grabbed the back of her neck and propelled her ahead of him down to the creek and over to a flat rock that projected out into the water. He pushed her down roughly, then sat down beside her.

Little Dove was astonished, crying. Too much was happening and she didn't know how to deal with it. What had happened to Grandfather? Why was he so angry?

Grandfather sat quietly for a while, letting her calm down and his own temper subside. He still held the cross with its broken cord in his hand.

"Little Dove," he finally said, "this cross you were wearing represents the destruction of our people. It makes me very sad to see you wearing it. We have already lost your brother. We had to banish him from the kiva society because he was insulting the elders, the old ones, the *kachinas*, the gods themselves. He kept insisting that we were all going to hell— whatever that means—because we don't follow his *Cristo*. I weep for him. But he is young and may some day return to his senses.

"I weep for you, too, because I understand the lure of the mission. I don't want to lose you, too. When you wear this cross, it cuts you off from all we have known and loved over the generations. And it will put you in danger because many of our people are becoming more resistant to the *gachupines* and the missions."

Out of his pouch he extracted an ancient bone bead with a neck cord attached.

"You have to decide, Little Dove. I ask you to wear this bone bead, a gift from the ancestors, to help you remember who you are, a child of the proud Cicuye. And here is your cross, symbol of the Spanish way of life. They are different. One will connect you with our ancestors and all we hold sacred. The other will separate you from us, taking you into a different and alien world. Which will you choose?"

He took her hand, patted her head and embraced her with emotion. Then he stood up and walked away.

Little Dove sat there beside the creek, the cross in one hand and the bone bead in the other, tears rolling down her cheeks.

BONG! A sound split the air. BONG! BONG! The nearby ravens flew up in fright and winged off toward the mesa top. BONG! BONG! BONG! BONG! The hum of activity at the pueblo became silent. BONG! BONG! BONG! BONG! The men had finally hung the bell and were trying it out. Its voice resounded all through the valley, echoing off the nearby cliffs, making vibrations that shivered the skin. It was announcing, "*CRISTO* IS HERE!" BONG! BONG! BONG! BONG!

The sound stabbed at her heart. Who was she to be? Little Dove or Palomita? Cicuye or Pecos? A follower of the gods of earth and sky, or of the new *Cristo* who hung on the cross? A member of her ancient community, or of the entrancing new one?

She didn't know. Confused, her tears joined company with the waters of the creek that had flowed forever, giving life to her people.

6

After the Spanish Left (1681 AD)

SHELL TRUDGED WEARILY down the path from the mesa. In the net carry-bag over her shoulder she carried a small pot that had held beans and chile and some stringy roots she had dug up with her pointed digging stick. The ground was very dry and dust squirted up beneath her bare toes.

Below her, the terraced building of the great Pecos Pueblo squatted solidly on the ridge. She could see people moving in and out, working at their various tasks. In one of the garden plots beside the creek, she could see Father trying to coax continued life out of the scraggly corn plants, dripping pots full of water on each one with hopeful care. There were no piñons this year. Many of the crops had dried up, the wheat fields beyond the mission were mere stubble, and the deer had retreated far into the mountains. Shell and all her people were hungry.

Her mind whirled in confusion. In some ways everything seemed the same, but it was all so different. The great white church at the end of the ridge was now just a huge pile of rubble destroyed by angry Indians. The priests, the kindly old one and the lively young one, along with several of their mission helpers and converts, were dead, killed by furious mobs. The big bronze bell had disappeared. The Spaniards were gone, those not killed in the uprising fleeing to the south.

Angry Pecos men and women had destroyed the church, had speared the sheep, uprooted fruit trees, thrown metal tools into the creek, ripped up books and woolen cloth, killed cows and oxen and donkeys, smashed two-wheeled carts. *Get rid of everything the Spaniards brought, and we'll really be free from their hated tributes and forced labor on their ranches and interference in our religious ceremonies and dances. Let everything be as it was before they came. Then we can honor our gods in the old ways, the rains will return, the animals will come back, we'll keep the work of our hands and the goods brought in trade, and we'll live again in harmony with the earth.*

That's what they said. That's what Popé, the great medicine man, had told them. Shell wanted to believe it, but she couldn't. She couldn't imagine life without chickens and steel knives and needles and wheat bread baked in the round-topped ovens and chile and chocolate and the sound of the great bell echoing over the valley in times of joy or sorrow. No longer should she speak Spanish. She used to have two names: Concha in Spanish and Shell in the Pecos language. They meant the same thing, but now she was allowed only the one.

Screaming and shouting and running around—that's what she remembered from the day it all happened. The uprising against the Spaniards had been planned for a long time, and most of the other pueblos had joined together under the leadership of Popé. Her father and older brother had been in the middle of the turmoil, but in the confusion nobody was quite sure who sided with whom. Grandfather had ordered her and her mother to take the new baby brother and hide. For a while, they had huddled in one of their storerooms. Then they managed to sneak out of the pueblo and clamber to a place on the mesa where other women and children had gathered

Then Father went off with other warriors to Santa Fe where surviving colonists and soldiers were trapped in the fortified government palace. Popé was there, encouraging a huge number of warriors from many pueblos. This was the first time they had agreed on anything and had come together against a common enemy. Some of the warriors had guns or the hard leather vests like many of the soldiers wore, and they waved silken banners stolen from the homes they had looted. But Father, like most of the fighters, had only their bows and arrows and war clubs.

At one point, the Spanish soldiers had surged out of the gateway on their horses, swinging their swords and battle axes. Many pueblo warriors were killed in that fight, including Father's brother and his best friend. Father came home soon afterwards with a deep gash on his arm from a Spanish sword. It still hadn't healed. Father was gloomy, silent and seldom spoke to anybody. He spent the daylight hours working among his plants, trying to encourage life after experiencing so much death.

The people of the pueblo were bitterly divided. Some had been eager to drive out the Spaniards after suffering years of many kinds of abuse. Others felt more kindly toward the Spanish settlers and the mission priests. They spoke Spanish and had adopted much of—though not all—of the religion of the mission, adapted the new foods, tools and animals to their own uses. Many had become friends with some of the settlers and tried to protect them and the two respected priests from the killing rage. In vain. The Pecos governor was one of these. In fear for his life, he was hiding somewhere in the hills for the time being.

As of now, it seemed that the Spanish-haters, urged on by Popé, were in control of the pueblo. They swaggered, threatened and intimidated the others, sometimes with violence. Nobody felt safe anymore. Old friends avoided each other, families were split apart with conflict. Elders, like Grandfather who tried to restore harmony, were mocked by one side or the other, or both. It was a terrible time.

～

Shell splashed through the creek at the base of the pueblo's rocky ridge, but there was hardly enough water in it to splash. She wondered where she could find Grandfather in a place she could talk with him alone. She had an important secret to share, and she needed his advice.

She had taken the little food her mother could spare to her older brother, Turkey Feather. He and a friend were tending a small flock of sheep, goats and a couple of donkeys far back on the mesa in hopes that Popé's followers would not find and destroy them. Her brother was one of many people who were hiding or retrieving Spanish goods that were now officially forbidden, but that the Pecos people had come to depend on. Normally, Shell would not have ventured alone so far into wild country, but these were not "normal" times. She had watched carefully for strangers or for other Pecos people who might prove hostile, hiding in shallow arroyos or diving into clumps of bushes whenever a person came into sight.

The watchman on the roof beside the gateway shouted a greeting. He usually teased her and she teased right back, but today she wasn't in the mood. Where was Grandfather?

There he was! Over in a corner of the big plaza! A group of husky warriors, wild young men she knew, surrounded him. He looked so small and wizened compared to them, yet he stood straight and his voice was strong. Shell drew near to hear what they were saying. She could see that Grandfather was very angry by the way his jaw twitched. Usually, his anger made him silent, but these were not "usual" times.

"You young warriors boast and brag, but you don't use your heads," he was saying. "You have often told how you went to the ranch of don Francisco and killed him, his wife, his children and his servants. You then killed the animals, burned the buildings, destroyed everything you could . . ."

"He deserved it," one of the young warriors growled. "He had enslaved us for years, taking our crops, our hides, our blankets, our piñons, our labor, our women. He was an evil man!"

"That may be so, but that's not the point." There was an edge to Grandfather's voice. "What was in his storerooms? <u>Our</u> corn and beans. <u>Our</u> cotton and wool blankets and carefully tanned deerskins and buffalo robes. <u>Our</u> pottery and jewelry, the work of <u>our</u> hands. All of which he would send to the south to trade and sell for his own profit. We, your people, are hungry and cold. Did you remember us? <u>No</u>! You burned everything up into smoke and ashes. How about the animals? Horses, oxen, mules, donkeys, sheep, goats, chickens? All dead, with not a piece of hide or a feather left for us. How about the wagons, the carts, the tools he had there? Didn't you think that <u>we, your people</u>, could use them? And you destroyed the fruit trees and the crops in the fields that had been carefully tended with our labor!"

The young warriors began to look ashamed. One, who was digging his toes into the dust of the plaza, muttered defensively, "But Popé says we need to destroy everything the Spaniards brought, and only then will we be free. Then the Ancient Ones will bless us <u>again</u>."

"Um hum," replied Grandfather. "I've known you since you were children. You have no idea what it was like before the Spaniards came. Think about it. Some of the things they brought us are very good indeed. Those big yellow peaches, sweet and juicy, that you like so much, for instance. The chile that bites the tongue and spices our stews. The sweet chocolate drink that strengthens and delights. The woolen blankets so soft and warm on our backs. The chickens and their eggs you like to eat, particularly when the hunts are not successful. The steel knives so useful for cutting. Do you remember how to make such tools from stone? How about the donkeys that carry our loads, and the wheat bread baking in our ovens in the morning, and the guns the soldiers use to help fight our enemies? I could go on . . .

"Yes, there was much evil in the way many of the Spanish *gachupines* treated us. But not all of them were like that. It is good that they have gone. But that's no reason to destroy the good things they brought us."

"Old man, you don't know what you are talking about!" One of the warriors flung a challenge

"Young man," Grandfather retorted, "now, *you* are talking like a Spaniard yourself. The pueblo way, the Pecos way, *our* way is to speak with *respect* to our elders."

He turned and stomped away while the young warriors, abashed, wandered off.

⌒

Shell saw Mother waving at her from her upper terrace, so she clambered up the ladder to take her the empty pot and the roots. The storerooms, usually so full of food and other good things, were almost empty. Still, Mother had a pot of beans simmering on the fire and some corn meal mush already prepared. Mother looked worn and anxious. The baby was sleeping. Hungry, Shell gobbled up a gourdful of the mush with bits of chile in it.

But she needed to talk with Grandfather and soon returned to the plaza. She found him sitting on a mat, slumped against a wall, looking exhausted. Looking at him, she remembered the many winter nights when the family and friends huddled around their small fire while icy winds howled around the sheltering stone walls. At those times, Grandfather's stories helped the time pass quickly. He told of the times before the Spaniards came, as he had been told by his parents and grandparents, and about the building of the great church before he was born. He described with delight the trade fairs at the pueblo, about his travels to far-off places, and the people who came and went. He mentioned with respect the leaders who had influenced his life and with chuckles some of the events he himself had experienced. He set them all to laughing at the strange actions and beliefs of many of the Spanish settlers who, though often feared or hated, said and did things the pueblo people thought were very funny. When you can laugh at them, they don't seem quite so terrible. He had gained a lot of wisdom over the years and was one of the most respected of the Pecos elders. But now he looked old and tired.

⌒

Concerned, she touched his arm. "Are you all right, Grandfather?"

"Hello, Granddaughter. I'm just a little tired. These are difficult times we live in."

"Grandfather, I need to talk with you in private. Nobody must hear us."

"Look, Granddaughter. People are gathering around the kiva over there. They are going to hear the news that a runner brought this morning. Popé himself will visit us in two days' time. We need to get ready, but I doubt that Popé will be able to bring together our divided community. Nobody will hear us here. Speak."

"Grandfather, you know that Turkey Feather is up on the mesa with a flock of sheep and goats, trying to keep them safe."

The old man nodded.

"Do you remember the Spanish women and children who were staying at the *convento* waiting for their husbands to return when, when the killing started?"

"Yes. I believe they were all killed."

"Not all of them. Turkey Feather found one woman with two small children who had escaped to the mesa. She was wandering alone, starving, trying to look after her little ones. Turkey Feather at first thought he should kill them because they are Spaniards. Then he thought he should not because the woman was so brave, and one of the small ones smiled at him. So he gave them milk from one of the goats and took them to a rock shelter in a small ravine where they could stay hidden out of the sun and the wind. He killed a young sheep, dried some of the meat and roasted the rest in a fire pit for them. The woman scraped the hide so the children could lie on the soft wool. He has been sharing the food we bring him and hunting for whatever he can find for them. But they are hungry and the nights are getting cold. Turkey Feather wants to know what he should do. Kill them? Abandon them? Continue to help them however he can? Please advise him.

Grandfather sat silent with his eyes closed for so long that Shell thought he must have gone to sleep. Finally, he opened his eyes and looked at her. He pulled off his necklace and slipped it over Shell's head. It was a handsome string of lumps of turquoise and little shells surrounding a large, ancient bone bead. There was no other like it in the pueblo. Grandfather always wore it, and everybody knew it was his.

"Take this to Hawk Tail," he said. "You'll find him in the *convento*, what's left of it. He is in charge of the supplies still stored there, the food and blankets and much more, which he distributes to needy families as long as they last. Ask him, in my name, for two wool blankets, a measure of corn meal and one of beans. This necklace will prove that you come from me. Take these things to the Spanish woman and tell her to wear this necklace where all can see it. Any Pecos person who finds her will know that she is under my protection. It may help her survive, or maybe not. After Popé leaves the area, we'll see if there is anything we can do for her, but I don't know what will happen. We've had enough killing already. And you might tell your friend Lupe to head for the mesa for the next few days.

⌒

Lupe lived in the part of the pueblo nearest to the now-ruined church. Though her mother was a Pecos, her father was a Spanish settler who worked on a ranch near Santa Fe. He had a Spanish wife, but came to visit Lupe and her mother often. Sometimes he brought them special gifts—a large chunk of chocolate, some fine porcelain cups, a length of velvet cloth. No one knew if he had been killed in the uprising, or if he had escaped with the surviving Spaniards.

Shell thought Lupe was beautiful in a strange way. Though her features resembled the Pecos people, her skin was a golden tan and her hair a frizzy brown instead of straight black. She had astonishing green eyes that sparkled with interest and humor about everything around her. The jokes she made about herself and others like her, with the confusion of being neither Spanish nor Indian, kept her friends laughing and loving her. But she was so obviously of mixed parentage that her life was in danger at this time. She had been hiding, keeping out of sight since the uprising began. But Shell knew where to find her and easily persuaded her to go with her to the mesa.

⁓

Before daylight, the two girls crept out of the pueblo, past the sleepy guard, carrying supplies and food in their net carry-bags. Up on the mesa, few people were stirring and easily avoided by the wary girls. Eventually, they found Turkey Feather who led them over rough country to a small ravine. A careful call, a soft answer, and they approached the overhanging rock shelter.

The Spanish women seemed shy and nervous until Lupe spoke to her in rapid, soft Spanish, bringing out the good things they had brought her. For the children, there were even some pieces of *piloncillo,* the hard brown sugar brought on the *Camino Real* some time ago. The little one was still a baby who watched the visitors blankly while sucking at his mother's dried-up breast. The older one appeared to be sick. Snot ran out of his nose while he grabbed hold of Turkey Feather's finger and chattered incomprehensiously. The mother was thin and anxious. She didn't know where her husband was, if he had heard about the uprising, if he would ever find her again. Her dress was tattered and torn and an ugly sore on her foot had not healed. She welcomed the gourd of goat milk Turkey Feather had brought and thanked the girls effusively for the gifts. She almost smiled when she said, "Maybe they will help us live a little longer."

Shell felt shy and uneasy in her presence, unsure of how she should show the respect she felt for the woman's courage. Clumsily, she draped Grandfather's necklace around her neck while Lupe described its purpose. Lupe stayed to visit and to help her for a little while. Shell made her way back to the pueblo.

Later that day, the watchers on the rooftops sent up a cry, "Riders coming!" People swarmed up the ladders to look. Horsemen were approaching the pueblo, a large number of them.

In the lead rode a strange figure on a fine black stallion. An Indian, he wore a shining Spanish helmet and a flowing red velvet cape pinned with a large silver ornament. On his bare chest thick strings of turquoise bounced with the motions of the horse. White deerskin moccasins reached above his ankles. A Spanish sword swung at his belt, and a single jingling spur was attached to one foot.

Shell recognized that his companions were Tewas from the pueblos along the Rio Grande. They carried guns and spears with metal tips and looked fierce. Shell knew that the Tewas, who lived closer to the Spanish settlements, had suffered more from the *gachupines* than the more distant Pecos had, and that most of them were strong supporters of Popé. But she felt nervous because the Tewas and the Pecos had never been friends.

Was it possible that the strange man with the red cape and the Tewa followers was the great Popé himself, the medicine man who had organized the revolt, unified the different pueblos and driven out the Spaniards?

It was and he was. The riders clattered into the plaza, almost filling it up. The elders came running out to greet them. Popé's eyes glittered and his voice was harsh. Yes, he told them, he had sent word that he would visit Pecos tomorrow, but he came today instead to see what his good friends, the Pecos people, were doing when they didn't expect them.

Many of the Pecos warriors surrounded Popé with delight. He was their hero! While big-eyed boys led the horses to the creek for water, the men proudly escorted Popé and his followers around the ridge top to show him what they had done. They inspected the ruined church and pointed to the spot where they would make a kiva in the *convento* area. They described the deaths of the priests and their closest followers, displayed a smashed cart, affirmed that they were removing all traces of the Spanish presence, and that later they would show how they had not forgotten the traditional dances. Not a animal brought by the Spanish was in sight. The ones that had been hidden away would soon be found and destroyed.

Shell, overhearing some of this, thought of Turkey Feather and the Spanish woman up on the mesa and wondered what would happen to Lupe if they found her. She knew that many women were quickly concealing their steel knives and copper pots, strings of chile and containers of chocolate. There might be big trouble if they were found. At one point, a stray chicken raced in front of the visitors. A Tewa snatched it up and wrung its neck, tossing the carcass to a dog. "Nothing Spanish here," he grunted, while Popé and his followers smiled approvingly.

The sound of drums and flutes lured them back to the plaza. Dancers emerged from the big kiva. They looked ragged, their feathers askew, and their dancing was slipshod because they had had almost no time for proper preparation, prayer and practice. Shell felt embarrassed for them. When finally they returned to the kiva, she helped the women distribute the feast, such as it was. So many strangers, so little food, so little time for preparation.

⌒

Finally, came the moment everyone had been waiting for. Shell joined the people crowding the terraces looking down at the events in the plaza. Popé stood on the rim of a kiva where all could see him. He was tall and lean with an expressive face. His voice rose and fell with drama and reached every corner of the plaza. He looked people in the eye and moved his hands for emphasis. It was easy to see how his words and passion could inspire so many followers.

Congratulations to his good friends, the Pecos, for their part in the uprising that drove away the evil Spaniards, he exulted. He recounted the injuries and abuses they had inflicted on the peaceful pueblo people for years and showed the marks of the Spanish whip that scarred his back. He recalled the time before the Spaniards came as one of peace, plenty and harmony with the spirits of the earth and sky. He urged the people to return to those times, to destroy all signs of the Spanish presence and the things they had brought.

So far, well and good. His listeners were attentive.

He pointed to a round-topped bread oven and shouted, "Smash it!" Three young Pecos warriors knocked it to pieces with rocks. One house had a carved wooden doorway; and on his command, his Pecos followers promptly broke it. He pointed in the direction of the orchards along the creek. "I can see you have destroyed some of the trees. Now get rid of the rest. We can live without the Spanish apples, peaches and pears!" Some people murmured assent, others looked distressed. No one moved to obey. He waved in the direction of the church. "The church is now in ruins. Good. But much of the *convento* still stands. Knock it down, burn everything inside." Shell could feel waves of resistance arising. The *convento* still had many uses, and the elders were carefully distributing the remaining supplies inside to families in need. And finally, after a long string of similar commands, Popé cried out, "Many of you accepted the water of baptism from the priests. Go down to the creek and scrub it off as if it had never happened. And if there are any among you here contaminated with Spanish blood, kill them, drive them away, make them your slaves."

Shell gritted her teeth and clenched her fists, glad that Lupe was safe upon the mesa. If anyone threatened her friend, she would protect her with her life!

Shell's skin prickled as she sensed undercurrents of antagonism. Popé was certainly a magical speaker. His words had power and many shared his vision. But among many others, resistance was growing. The tension was becoming explosive.

⌣

There was silence when Popé stopped speaking. His Tewa companions gathered around him, preparing to leave. Then a single voice rang out, loud and clear, and a small old man stepped up on the rim of the kiva. Shell saw with a mixture of pride and anxiety that it was Grandfather. Everybody stopped to listen.

"POPÉ!" he shouted, "you are a great warrior. You have accomplished what we all thought was impossible. You have brought together all our northern pueblos as one. Together, we drove out the *gachupines* who were oppressing us all. You have offered us your vision of a return to the Old Days when we lived in harmony with each other and with our gods. For this we give you our special thanks."

He paused for a moment and opened a small pouch of corn pollen. "Popé! May the spirits of our ancestors bless our words today!" He dipped his fingers into the pouch and scattered bits of corn pollen to the sacred directions.

Then he continued, "Popé! You have honored our Pecos pueblo and our people with your visit today. We have welcomed you and your Tewa companions. You have shared with us your desire for the elimination of everything the Spaniards brought us—the language, crops, tools, the animals, the faith in *Cristo*. Only when we are rid of all traces of those people will we be free. That is what you say. We have listened.

"But it does not seem that you heed your own words! You and your companions are riding fine Spanish horses, the same you wish to forbid to us. On your head you wear a shining Spanish helmet, while you would wish us to go into battle bareheaded. Your red cloak is of rich Spanish velvet, while for us you desire hand-woven cotton when we can trade for it, or tanned deerskins. A Spanish sword hangs by your side, yet you would have us abandon the steel knives so useful for our daily work. A Spanish spur adorns your heel, symbol of the *gachupines* who abused us so much. Your companions are carrying Spanish guns and lances tipped with steel, too good for our own warriors. You seem to be well fed, while our people go hungry. And because the many pueblo people speak in different languages and you speak our Pecos language imperfectly, you have been talking to us in Spanish which—fortunately—most of us still remember."

A murmur of protest surged through the crowd. This old man, one of the Pecos elders, had no fear of the mighty Popé! He was challenging him in a most unmannerly way. Some people were appalled, others relieved at the challenge that spoke for them. Shell held her breath as he continued.

"We Pecos, and the Cicuye before us, have always been a proud and independent people. As traders, we traveled far and wide and welcomed strangers to our pueblo. We have always considered new ideas, new tools, new ways of doing things, and we have adapted many of them into the life of our people. So it has been with the Spaniards among us for so many years. Some of them abused us, it is true. They tried to suppress our religion, our ceremonies and our gods. They didn't succeed. They brought us many new things ands taught us skills that have made our lives easier and richer. We made many friends among them.

"It is good that the *gachupines* have gone away, yet we mourn the lost lives of some of them. Many of the things they have left us are now part of our lives, not to be easily discarded. As we return to the ways of our ancestors, let us, in their tradition, keep these good things for the benefit of our people.

"And you, Popé! As I see the *gachupin* spur attached to your moccasin and hear your commands to return to past times, I wonder what is in your mind. Are you planning for us to exchange one kind of slavery for another—YOURS?"

An angry roar burst out from the crowd. People started yelling and shouting and shoving each other. The Tewas lowered their lances and readied their guns. Pecos warriors reached for their weapons.

A huge Tewa swung his fist at Grandfather's head. A young Pecos warrior blocked the blow, while another pulled Grandfather to safety. Shell noticed with surprise that these warriors were the same ones Grandfather had scolded so severely the day before.

But Popé was not ready for a fight. He leaped up on the edge of the kiva, raised his arms and shouted, "PEACE!" again and again. The tumult quieted He gathered his Tewas and moved toward the gateway. The horses were waiting. They mounted and rode away.

The arguments continued around the plaza, often bitterly, as the people debated the things they had heard. The elders and their helpers roamed around among them, trying to calm tempers before they came to blows.

⏝

It was almost dark when Father returned from the fields. His arm was hurting, his heart was grieving for good friends killed, and he wanted nothing to do with Popé. He slumped down beside Grandfather on the terrace, their backs leaning against the wall. Shell brought them bowls of thick soup and lingered to listen to what they were saying.

Exhausted, Grandfather was describing Popé's visit. "We have survived difficult times, but I fear more are coming. Conflict within our pueblo and conflict with others like Popé's Tewas will bring more killing and more sorrow. And of course, when the Utes and Apaches see us so divided, they will raid us again and again. Perhaps the Spaniards will return, eager for vengeance and to reclaim their northern settlements. What will we do then? We'll need all of our courage, endurance and wisdom."

Father gloomily scooped up a bit of soup with a piece of tortilla. "I wish I had more of all three of those things," he lamented. "Maybe in time they'll return to me."

Later, Lupe crept back through the darkened pueblo. Shell rejoiced to see her friend unharmed. She described the day's events and warned Lupe that she was not yet out of danger.

⏝

The next morning, Turkey Feather appeared at the doorway. The Spanish woman had disappeared, he reported. There was no sign of her or of the children. The blankets and bean pot, the bags of meal and beans had gone with her—but where? He had tried to follow tracks, but the rocks in the ravine and the hardness of the surrounding land made it impossible. Had the Apaches found her and taken her away? Had her searching husband rescued her? Had Popé's men dragged her off to her death? Had Ute raiders captured her for a slave? He couldn't tell.

But he had found Grandfather's necklace hanging from a branch by the entrance to the rock shelter. He had brought it back, and he placed it carefully around Grandfather's neck where it belonged.

7

Was it a Bear? (1760 AD)

DOES GOD EVER LAUGH? Carapicada pondered the thought while the young priest droned on and on. Automatically, at the signals from the *fiscales*, the priest's helpers, she stood or knelt on the hard dirt floor of the church and repeated the expected responses of the liturgy.

Our Lady of the Angels, the Virgin María. The painting over the altar portrayed the lovely woman with golden halo reaching one hand invitingly out toward the viewers, while little angels played at her feet. The picture usually inspired and comforted her.

She had been baptized María in her honor, but now everybody called her Carapicada, Pock Face. Today, she imagined the little angels flapping their wings and buzzing around the Virgin like mosquitoes. Would she move her upraised arm pointing toward Heaven to swat at them? The idea made her giggle.

The *Cristo* on the cross, on the other hand, with blood dripping from his wounds, didn't offer much to laugh at. But maybe the joke was on the men who had tried to kill him. He didn't stay dead. That was funny, too.

The regular priest was away in Santa Fe, and this young one who had been sent to replace him temporarily looked as if he had forgotten how to laugh, if he had ever known how. His colorful vestments and the candles, the incense and the holy sacrament that gave him a certain spiritual power over the lives of the Pecos people didn't seem to give him much joy. Maybe he was nervous because he didn't know what to expect here. Maybe he was afraid of the Comanches.

Father used to insist that laughter helped people survive hard times. There had been plenty of hard times here lately, yet he had always managed to see the humorous side of things. He had often served as one of the *koshare*, the sacred clowns, at the pueblo religious dances. While the singers' voices and the throbbing drums and the dancers' feet and bodies moved in unison in the age-old ceremonies that reconnected the people with the ancient spirits of the place, the *koshare* made people laugh. Their bodies were painted with black and white stripes, and their antics, rude comments, and silly jokes set watchers giggling and roaring with delight. It was part of a long tradition. Father was one of the best.

Would he have found anything funny about the Comanche raid that killed him? A stab of grief shot through her heart.

~

The priest had mounted the steps to the pulpit and was now preaching to the people in Spanish. For many years, none of the priests had learned the Pecos language, not even a few words of greeting. Carapicada could understand and speak Spanish pretty well—Grandfather had seen to that—so usually she had a fair idea of what was going on. But sometimes she preferred to pretend she didn't understand, like when the bishop was asking her too many questions on his visit a few months ago. She quietly giggled when she heard the bishop scolding the regular priest for not learning the language.

She tried to listen to the young priest's sermon but wasn't making much sense as far as she could tell. One of the *fiscales*, Bernardo, was translating, but he wasn't making much sense either. Or was he? In the rhythm of the priest's words, Bernardo's message was quite different. Amidst a lot of gobbledygook he was telling the people, "Tomorrow stay home. Prepare food. Go to the plaza. Something will happen." A sly sparkle lit up his eyes.

The listening people didn't move a muscle, apparently absorbed in the sermon and the mass. But Carapicada noticed that those eyes she could see also sparkled. That was funny, she thought, and she giggled again.

A small commotion at the door attracted her attention but she couldn't see its cause. Suddenly a raucous "Cock-A-Doodle-Doo" split the air. Twisting her head, she glimpsed a huge red rooster, a truly handsome bird, strutting down the aisle toward the altar.

"Catch it!" shouted Bernardo. Hands reached out to capture it, but Carapicada could tell that they were intentionally missing or gently pushing the bird ahead. People started to laugh and to cackle and crow like chickens.

The priest stopped preaching and stood transfixed, not knowing how to deal with the intruder. The boys in the choir started making silly comments. One reached out for a bit of communion bread and held it out. With another loud "Cock-A-Doodle-Doo", the rooster flapped his wings and landed on the altar, gobbling up the communion bread. Bernardo and the priest tried to grab it but missed, and the bird scampered out of reach, flapped to the top of the pulpit and on up to one of the roof beams. By now, the whole congregation and the two *fiscales* were roaring with laughter.

The priest's efforts to regain control were useless. Finally, he shouted above the tumult, "<u>Amen</u>!" and slunk out the side door.

What a good time Father would have had with this! Carapicada thought. She wondered if her brother, Gray Eyes, had been involved. She suspected he had.

～

As she walked out the door, Carapiada paused to look up at the high walls and twin towers of the church. It was nestled among the stone foundations of the much larger church that had been destroyed during the uprising. The old folks told stories they had heard from their grandparents about the great white church with its six towers and its pealing bells that resounded over the valley, and about the priests, some loved and some merely endured, who had taught the people so many new things. They described the huge interior with glorious music, bright candles, and colored robes that gave warmth and light to the dimness. Some had helped paint the vivid pictures of the *santos* looking down from the walls and had taken part in the dramatic ceremonies and symbolic acts that were somehow very powerful, whether or not they were understood.

They also talked about the heavy burdens imposed on the Pecos community to support this church, as well as tribute for the faraway king of Spain, whoever that might be. The work of their hands their crops, the hides they tanned, their woven cotton and woolen blankets, fine pottery, baskets of piñon nuts and so much more disappeared in the wagons of the authorities. In spite of the resentment of the forced labor on Spanish farms and workshops, there were many funny stories about mishaps, misunderstandings, and the strange Spanish customs encountered through the work.

They remembered Spaniards, good and bad, driven away by the uprising for a while, that were welcomed by some and resisted by others when they returned. And they pondered the constant struggle to keep alive the ancient traditions that ensured harmony with the spiritual powers of the universe. This present church, constructed after the return of the priests, was much smaller than the earlier one because so many of the Pecos people had died or moved away.

Outside the carved doors, small groups of people were talking animatedly. Some were laughing, others seemed angry at the disrespect for God's sacred mass and feared reprisals. It was clear that not everybody appreciated the joke about the rooster.

One of the Spanish soldiers whose name was Lorenzo was leaning against a wall cleaning his fingernails with the tip of his knife. He winked at her in a friendly way. She noticed and ignored him. He was one of six soldiers who had been assigned to protect the mission and the pueblo from raiders. They had built a fortified tower, a *torreón*, into a wall of the *convento* from which they could watch for intruders and shoot at them. But the Comanches generally came and went too fast for their guns to be effective. Lorenzo and his Indian wife and baby lived in the *Casas Reales*, the government apartments built for them just outside the mission.

Near the *convento*, on the far side of the church, she noticed mules with large packs and some strange white men who did not look Spanish. They were talking with the soldiers, and she wondered if they were the *franceses* she had heard about.

‌⁓

Walking toward her home on the Great Plaza, Carapicada looked at the many apartments now unoccupied in some of the house blocks. Several of them were falling down because no one was caring for them. She wondered vaguely if anything useful could still be found in them that had not yet been carried off.

"Prepare food." Bernardo's instruction floated back into her mind. Mother would need help. Poor Mother! She seemed tired all the time, sad, and she never smiled or joked the way she used to. She had had a hard time over the past few years.

There were the dry seasons when the rains didn't come and the crops withered and the people had to struggle to feed the Spaniards and visiting Apache allies, as well as themselves. They were often hungry. During this time, Baby Brother was born, but he was sickly and Mother was slow to regain her strength.

Then the Comanche raids increased, and people were afraid to venture far from the protecting walls of the pueblo and the mission. Yet they still had to tend their fields and gather firewood and herd the sheep and travel between the pueblo and Santa Fe and ranches for business or for their assigned work. The Comanches didn't raid often, but they came suddenly, dashing in on their horses before the watchers on the cliffs could give the alarm, and disappearing as quickly as they had arrived, leaving death and destruction in their wake. Carapicada knew every hole and hollow in the area where she could hide like a frightened rabbit if necessary. In spite of the handful of soldiers stationed at the mission and the skills of their own warriors, everybody was tense and nervous.

Then the great sickness that returned every few years struck again. Carapicada was one of its victims. She remembered days and nights lying helpless on her mat, shivering, sweating, aching all over, barely conscious of the people tending her and of what was happening around her. When her awareness returned and her head cleared, she was covered with itchy scabs that eventually fell off, leaving deep scars, particularly on her face.

She had survived, but with great sorrow she learned that Grandmother, Mother's wise and much loved mother, and Baby Brother had both died of the disease. Though Mother cared for her tenderly, she looked so exhausted and sorrowful that Carapicada thought that her heart would break.

But that wasn't all. Mother's two sisters and best friend, with their families, moved away to Santa Fe and other pueblos. They had always provided assistance and companionship, sharing stories and laughter, gossip and wisdom, along with the unending work. Mother felt lonely and abandoned.

And the Comanches killed Father. Mother had taken from Father's body his prize necklace of polished turquoise and pieces of shell surrounding the large bone bead said to come from the ancestors. She wore it constantly herself. It gave her comfort and courage from the ancient people, she said. But her grieving was intense. Carapicada tried to help her in every way she could—in the home, in the fields (which had been Father's job), with the weaving and preparing hides, making pottery and in the countless domestic tasks needed every day.

⏜

She rubbed the pitted scars on her face reflectively. It was Father who had helped her deal with them. She had gone with him and Mother to Santa Fe, riding in the oxcart on top of the load of wood he was taking to his brother who worked as a carpenter in the town. While Father and Mother gossiped inside, she had gone outside to wait for them in the oxcart.

A group of local children had stopped in their play to stare at her. "*Carapicada! ¿Qué te pasó?*" one of them had taunted. "Pock Face! What happened to you?" She tried to tell them that her name was María, but they started teasing her. "*Fea, fea, fea,*" they shouted. "Ugly, ugly, ugly! You'll never get a sweetheart, you ugly creature! Pock Face! *Carapicada!*"

By the time Father came out and the children ran away, she was huddled in the bottom of the *carreta*, her arms wrapped around her head, her shoulders shaking with sobs. Father pulled her upright and studied her face. "They're right, you know. You <u>are</u> a *carapicada*. Your face will never look like it used to. But you are a Pecos, one of a strong and brave people. You are a survivor. The pockmarks are a badge of honor. You are still you, with your life before you. You can live with joy and wisdom with much to give to our people. And you are <u>our</u> *carapicada*. CA-RA-PI-CA-DA!" He sounded the word out several times in different ways. Once it sounded musical, then like galloping horses, then like a love song, then squeakily comical. She finally had to laugh along with him. The name stuck. She giggled at the memory. The joke was on the horrid children who had tried to insult her.

⌒

She found Mother sitting outside her doorway mending Grandfather's moccasins. She sat down beside her and told about the rooster, about Bernardo's strange message and about the pack mules at the *convento*. Mother listened with interest but didn't have much to say. So Carapicada filled the water jar, brought in some armloads of wood from the pile just outside the gateway up the ladder to the terrace, ground some corn, mended a broken basket, brought out food from the dwindling supply in the storeroom and tended the cooking fire. Mother was sorting beans for simmering in the big black bean pot with whatever flavorings she had available.

⌒

Later, Carapicada climbed the ladder to the roof. Her brother Gray Eyes was chipping stone points and fastening them to the shafts of new arrows. His strange light eyes, inherited from some long forgotten Spanish ancestor, gave him a distinctive appearance.

She sat down near him. It was hard to come up here where Father had died. The Comanches, approaching among the trees where the cliff-top watchers couldn't see them, had suddenly dashed out at daybreak, whooping and yelling, racing their horses round and round the ridge where both the pueblo and the mission were rooted. They shot their arrows and their few guns at the warriors on the rooftops and the soldiers on the *torreón*, who replied with arrows, spears, stones, and a few bullets. They galloped off as suddenly as they arrived, taking with them a large part of the pueblo horse herd. Five people lay dead: two men and a woman caught outside the pueblo walls, a child hit by a stray arrow as he was running across the plaza—and Father.

Father, awakened from sleep, was on the rooftop. As he reached around for more arrows for his bow, a Comanche arrow thudded into his back. He died soon after. His friends and family wrapped him in his sleeping mat and buried him tenderly with all the proper ceremonies in the soft ground just below the pueblo's east wall. He had been much loved by all.

Carapicada wished he had had time to put on the hard leather vest the Spaniards had given him. Made of several layers of tough hide, it could deflect most arrows so they bounced off. Father had ridden out with the militia—a mixed group of Spanish soldiers, settlers, and pueblo warriors—to hunt the Comanches out on the plains. They had given him a good horse, a long lance with steel point and red tassels and the protective vest, and they had set out with two carts full of supplies. Father had many funny stories about the expedition. They never found any Comanches, but they ate a lot of fresh buffalo meat. The vest that might have saved his life was out of reach in the carved chest inside the house.

⌒

She shook her head to banish the memories. "Did <u>you</u> take that rooster to church?" she asked Gray Eyes. He looked at her and grinned and changed the subject.

"Did you see those *franceses* in front of the *convento*? They're not supposed to be here, but their mules are carrying guns and ammunition. Our *soldados* want to trade with them instead of arresting them."

"How about you? Would you like one of those guns?"

"No way. They are heavy and slow and complicated. When the powder and bullets are gone, they are useless. Any good Indian can shoot arrows much faster and straighter than any old *frances* or *soldado* with a gun. Arrows are easy to make, and maybe these will kill a few Comanches."

"Do you know what's going to happen tomorrow?"

Gray Eyes only grinned and looked away. "Father was a great *koshare*," he observed.

The ladder creaked and Grandfather clambered up onto the roof. He sat down on his usual piece of log. His eyes searched the horizon, but he said nothing. Gray Eyes and Carapicada waited respectfully. When he had something to say, he would say it.

At last he addressed Gray Eyes. "Grandson, I have heard that you were the one who brought the rooster to mass in the church today."

Carapicada noticed that Gray Eyes lowered his head. She suspected that he had many comments on the tip of his tongue, but he kept silent out of respect for his elder. But Carapicada spoke up eagerly. "Grandfather, were you there? Did you see how funny it was?"

Gray Eyes gave her a warning look. Her enthusiasm interrupting Grandfather's question to her brother was rude.

Grandfather spoke sharply, "Mind your manners, girl. Grandson, Granddaughter, it is not good to mock the gods, even those who are not ours. When Don Diego de Vargas brought the Spaniards back to our land after the uprising, many of our Pecos warriors helped him gain control over other pueblos. In return, he gave our Pecos people special privileges, and we have been friends with the Spaniards ever since. Their god and their priests no longer interfere with our own religious beliefs, and we are free to hold our dances and ceremonies in the old ways. But we must respect the priests and *Cristo* for the good things they bring us. Don Diego de Vargas, rest his soul, was my godfather. The Spaniards have treated us fairly. When the soldiers' pigs ruined my corn crop, the Governor himself ordered them to fence them in properly and to give me two of them to pay for the damage. The law respects us Indians."

Carapicada and Gray Eyes looked at each other and smothered giggles. On every possible occasion, Grandfather spoke of Don Diego de Vargas as his godfather and told the story of the pigs. It was totally predictable.

Gray Eyes spoke politely. "Grandfather, you say we mustn't mock the gods. But isn't that part of our long Pecos tradition? Isn't that how the *koshare* have always made us laugh? And Father too?"

"Grandson, think again. It's not the *gods* the *koshare* mock."

"Grandfather, the rooster was so funny . . . and the expression on the priest's face . . ." Carapicada was speaking, but Gray Eyes interrupted with an angry edge to his voice.

"Yes, Grandfather, the Spaniards no longer interfere with our religious practices, but they keep us so busy working for them in their fields and ranches and workshops, tending their crops and animals, tanning hides and weaving blankets and building houses and carving furniture and making pots and gathering piñons, that we have no time for our own ceremonies and proper preparation for them and barely enough for our own survival. No wonder the Comanches come instead of the rains. Many of our Pecos people do not feel as friendly toward the Spaniards as you do. As you have told us often, the Spaniards and their missions have brought great troubles and conflicts among us, and many of our people have left Pecos and gone elsewhere because of this."

"Be careful, Grandson, of what you do and say."

Carapicada felt embarrassed at the unusual emotion behind the words and didn't dare look at either. Both sat in silence for a while. Finally, Grandfather stood up and went down the ladder, while Gray Eyes bit his lip and went back to his arrows.

～

The next day dawned bright and crisp with the special clear light of early fall that makes the mountains sparkle. The crops were ripening in the fields, and the people were hopeful that this year the harvest would be plentiful in spite of the Comanches. Soon, visitors from other pueblos and plains tribes would be gathering here for the annual trade fair. The few Comanches that arrived came in peace, though sometimes the guns they traded for were used in raids on the pueblos the next week

As soon as she woke up, Carapicada was aware of a special excitement in the air. Someone had built a brush shelter, its roof adorned with green branches, at one end of the plaza. People were lounging around, sitting in the sun, smoking, chatting, waiting for—they didn't know what. The smell of good wheat bread in the round-topped *hornos* scented the air.

At last, someone called out from a rooftop, "Riders coming!"

Carapicada scampered up the ladder to have a look. "The bishop is coming back!" she shouted down to Mother. "I thought he had gone back south after his visit last spring."

Mother joined her and watched the approaching procession. Four Spanish soldiers with long lances were in the lead riding their best horses. A crowd of Indians followed. In between the two groups came three men riding donkeys. The one in the middle wore a bishop's mitre on his head and an elaborate cloak. He carried a curved staff of office, and a large painted cross bounced against his chest. On one side rode a man in a blue robe such as the Franciscan missionaries wore. On the other side rode a black man, surely the servant that accompanied the bishop everywhere. But something was wrong.

Mother started to laugh, for the first time in months, Carapicada thought. "That's not the bishop! It's Agustín the carpenter, the *koshare* companion of your father's. Let's see what he's going to do."

⌒

Carapicada followed Mother down the ladder to the plaza where they joined the other people gathering around the entrance. Drums started to throb and some flutes played solemn tunes as the procession entered the pueblo. The soldiers were the local ones. Lorenzo, with a big grin on his face, was in the lead. As she looked carefully at the black man, she recognized Bernardo, the *fiscal*, with his face and hands blackened with charcoal. Then she spotted Gray Eyes leading the Indian followers.

Upset by all the people crowding around, Bernardo's donkey bucked and tossed Bernardo off on his rear end and charged around the plaza braying frantically until someone caught him. The other donkeys were acting nervous, so the other two riders dismounted ungracefully, stumbling over their unfamiliar robes. They all looked so comical that everybody started laughing.

Without being told, the women formed two lines, making a pathway from the entrance to the brush shelter, just as they had done when the real bishop had visited. They knelt down and bowed their heads as "Bishop Agustín" walked between the rows, dumping "holy water" on their heads and "blessings" and a couple of rude comments about each one as he passed. Agustín had observed the bishop well. He mimicked and exaggerated the bishop's every gesture, every mannerism, even his way of speaking, to the delight of his appreciative audience. A large chair had been placed in front of the shelter, onto which Agustín lowered himself with great sighs and grunts.

The people gathered around as "Bishop Agustín," with great pomposity, waved his painted cross over the people and launched into a flowery speech, full of silly bits of theological distortions, misquotations from the mass, expressions in fake Latin and vague promises of strange foods for body and soul. It all made absolutely no sense, and the people loved it.

Then the blue-robed "priest" beside him proclaimed, "Now confessions will begin. You will each step up and confess your sins and receive the sacred absolution of Christ." Two of the respected elders were the first, then Gray Eyes, while everybody crowded closer to hear what they would say. One by one, many people knelt in front of the "bishop," each inventing more outlandish "confessions" than the last. In return, "Bishop Agustín" made ridiculous comments about the person, marked a wet, sloppy cross on their foreheads with water from a jar held by his "servant," and gave them a hearty smack on the side of the head. Each exchange was greeted with loud cheers and gales of laughter from the bystanders, as more of them lined up for the "ritual." Even stray outsiders— the watching soldiers, a couple of Spanish settlers who had been passing by—were drawn in to participate whether or not they understood what was happening. Gray Eyes was obviously one of the organizers, and people were laughing until they hurt.

At last "Bishop Agustín" stood up and announced, "You have been very bad people. This is your penance. You must spend the rest of the day in feasting and dancing and enjoying yourselves."

Everybody cheered. Food was brought out. People ate and chatted and laughed. The tensions that had gripped the pueblo for so long relaxed. Chores and fears were forgotten. They smoked, gambled, played games of skill and chance, flirted, and tended to the children. Some brought out instruments from the church and played tunes learned from the Spaniards, including some of their own. Soon the dancing began, not the traditional religious dances but the informal social dances that involved everybody, young and old.

It was a happy time, thought Carapicada. She suspected that Grandfather disapproved. She had glimpsed him occasionally watching from one of the terraces, and she thought she recognized an occasional small smile. She wondered what the young priest was doing. He must be shocked, and she giggled a bit. But don't let the Comanches raid now, she prayed. Nobody would be ready to fight them. How the day would have delighted Father. From glimpses she had of Gray Eyes, she guessed he would carry on the *koshare* tradition.

⤶

The next day, the celebrations continued. This time, "Bishop

Agustín" preached a long and quite outrageous sermon. He switched back and forth between Spanish and the Pecos language with more bits of Latin from the mass thrown in. He made fun of the interpreters' mistranslations, and of the real bishop's insistence that the mission priests learn the local language and teach the locals proper Spanish. He made puns and jokes and silly remarks that sometimes concealed biting truths amidst the humor.

A "choir" of young men led by Gray Eyes, sang parodies of some of the psalms and hymns familiar from the mass, but with deliberately sour notes and pauses for satirical comments, while a drum thumped in the background. Then "Bishop Agustín" administered "communion," distributing bits of tortilla and bringing out more and more smacks on heads and shoulders. Mock anguished cries from the recipients and loud ridiculous complaints brought more joyous laughter from the bystanders.

Mother, Carapicada and the other women were kept busy preparing more food. Visitors from outside the pueblo came in to see what was happening, and some brought food to share. One Spanish settler had butchered a pig and brought in a huge tub of *chicharron*, delicious, crunchy pork rinds. Another had used much of the precious supply of sugar to make *biscochitos*, the cookie loved by all. Visiting Apaches brought dried buffalo meat. The Spanish soldiers had "borrowed" wheat flour from the mission storerooms with which the women baked loaves of tasty bread.

Lorenzo and another soldier brought out a guitar and a fiddle. They sang some of the songs from their faraway homeland, and then swung into the dance tunes played at the *fandangos* in Santa Fe and the big ranches in the area. Some of the Pecos people had learned these dances, and they imitated the steps and patterns with comical clumsiness. One of the visiting *franceses* borrowed the fiddle and played a lively tune while the other danced and pranced with such fast and fancy steps that his feet looked like blurs of motion. Then he grabbed one of the Pecos women and whirled her around to the music, to her great embarrassment and the delight of everybody else. It was all lively and fun with a joyous sense of shared community.

By the third day, the energy was diminishing. "Bishop Agustín" baptized some babies by holding them upside down and tickling their feet until they squealed and their mothers protested. People were tired, the food supplies were perilously low, and much work had been neglected for too long. Around midday "Bishop Agustín" and his attendants provided a final "blessing," mounted their donkeys and rode away. The people returned to their tasks, but now they were smiling, chuckling and sharing their observations and memories of all that had happened.

⌇

Two days later, Carapicada, Mother, Gray Eyes and some neighbors were sitting by the rooftop fireplace sharing a pot of squash soup and tortillas. It was a lovely evening with the slanting rays of the sun painting the landscape vivid colors. They could look down at the campground, where a few early arrivals for the trading fair had set up tipis. The scene was animated with the comings and goings. Comanches didn't raid trade fairs. They came to trade. Mother was smiling, chatting, almost her old self, though her hand frequently caressed Father's necklace with the old bone bead.

They were laughing at memories of "Bishop Agustín's" visit, anticipating the coming harvest that promised plentiful crops this season and would require an immense amount of work, remembering past trade fairs and wondering how many familiar folks would gather this year.

The ladder creaked and Grandfather clambered to the roof. His face was grim, his mouth set in a straight line, his eyes full of worry. He sat himself down on his usual log seat, and everybody waited patiently until he was ready to speak.

"Agustín is dead," he announced. A long pause while his listeners absorbed the news. "He had gone to work in his cornfields down by the river. He was tired and sat down to rest under a piñon tree. A bear came out of the woods and attacked him. It clawed and bit him many times. Then it ran back into the woods. His friend Mateo found him and called for help. Agustín died as they carried him back to the pueblo. But before he died, he confessed that the bear was God's way of punishing him for making fun of God's church."

⌒

The people sat in stunned silence. Many reactions raced through Carapicada's mind. What a strange bear, to attack someone who wasn't threatening him and then run off before feasting on the ripening corn! Was it really a bear, or two legged enemies of some sort? She knew that many people were upset at Agustín's portrayal of the bishop.

Did the Spanish god never laugh? Would he punish a man for bringing cheer and joy to a pueblo depressed by so many misfortunes? Was it a sin to restore life to Mother and probably other suffering people? Was the *koshare* tradition of Agustín and Father evil? What had Agustín really said? Was somebody, for whatever reason, twisting his words? Which god had more power, the god of *Cristo* or the pueblo deities who smiled on the ancient traditions?

She glanced at Gray Eyes whose head was down, absorbed in thought and grief for his friend Agustín. Grandfather looked upset, even though he had not approved of Agustín's burlesque. Mother clutched the bone bead on her necklace. What did it all mean?

There were no answers. The questions raged around in her head leaving her confused. Then she began to laugh, quietly, inside herself. Our Lady of the Angels, the lovely lady in the painting in the church, with her compassionate eyes and welcoming hand stretched out, must have told the god of *Cristo* about the sufferings of the Pecos people. The god who loved everybody, according to the priests, sent Agustín as his messenger to cheer the people in the old pueblo tradition. The bear, a powerful figure according to the same pueblo tradition, would never be used by a Christian god. Agustín had done a wonderful thing, bringing relief from their troubles, renewed connections with their pueblo heritage and a sense of hope for the future, for now life would surely improve.

Agustín had served his purpose, and his death by the bear, if that's what it was, would make him remembered, with all he stood for, as long as the Pecos people survived. He would never be forgotten. Maybe they'd make him a saint! She giggled again and she pictured the god of *Cristo* and the gods of the pueblo laughing together with compassion and caring, about this great fiesta that had brought healing and renewed life to Pecos.

Did this make any sense? She didn't know, though she suspected that neither the priest nor the pueblo elders would approve of her thoughts. What would Father have said? Maybe his spirit had brought these ideas that gave her comfort. And she felt a new kind of strength and energy filling her heart.

8

Departure—Where To? (1838 AD)

YOUNG CORN TRUDGED up the slope to the entrance of the old pueblo. She carried a huge squash in her arms and her back was bent under a large net bag full of corn. It was harvest time and she thought about her name. When she was little, had they called her "Corn Kernel" or "Corn Sprout"? Maybe as she grew older she would become "Corn Stalk" or "Dry Corn Husk" or "Tortilla."

She smiled at the thought and urged on her little brother in front of her. He was tired and dragged his feet, but he wouldn't let go of the round melon in his arms. He was especially precious. The Great Sickness last year had killed seven—almost all of the young children in the pueblo. There were only six or seven families living here now, and it was a catastrophic loss.

Some more rocks had fallen off the wall by the entrance. She wondered if anybody cared enough to anchor them back in place with mud.

She often felt sad when approaching the plaza. The place seemed so forlorn, falling apart. The few families still remaining had gathered at the north end of the great house block where the terraced rooms were still intact. Some of the other apartments, though abandoned, were still habitable, while others were crumbling. Outside of the plaza area heaps of stones marked where earlier houses had collapsed. Some of the rooms down near the church had been repaired and were occupied by the Old

Hermit and his son who tended a flock of goats up on the mesa. They traded goat milk and meat for tortillas and beans and helped watch over the church.

She remembered the stories the elders told of the old days when the pueblo teemed with activity with the comings and goings of all sorts of people, and Pecos was famous throughout the land for its extensive trade, its fine weaving and carpentry, its farmers and warriors, and its numerous and much respected people.

The church, once so full of light and life, was still standing. Some of the holy pictures and furnishings were still cared for there, but somebody had stolen the candlesticks, and the roof leaked because nobody bothered to repair it. The priest came over from San Miguel to say mass very rarely, only when a soldier escort could accompany him for fear of raiders from the plains. The *convento* was falling down, too. Her older brother, Piñon Boy, had just missed serious injury when a falling roof beam barely missed him.

Often she was angry, too. Angry that they were still living in this dreary place. There weren't enough people left to tend the fields and bring in the crops. The ceremonial dances, so vital to the well being of the pueblo, had been largely abandoned for lack of participants. Once flourishing sheep, cattle and horses now were reduced to two old mules, one scraggly burro and a dilapidated cart, as well as a few chickens and a couple of dogs. No longer a strong community, now they were victims of many forces around them. People like Mother had to work at nearby ranches to earn a hunk of beef or a warm blanket, or like Father who traded his carpentry skills for tools or sugar or sheepskins. Couldn't they go somewhere else where there were more people, more life, more joy? And more young people from whom she might eventually choose a husband?

⌒

Little brother stopped suddenly and she bumped into him. "Horsies," he announced. There were two of them with strange-looking saddles standing in the plaza with their heads down, their reins dragging on the ground. Over by the one remaining kiva two tall men were talking with small, wizened Grandfather. They wore big hats and sturdy boots and waved their hands wildly in efforts to communicate in bad Spanish. *Americanos!*

The one with the red beard and bright blue eyes looked familiar and friendly. He smiled at Young Corn and reached out to pick up Little Brother, melon and all, but the child yowled and hid behind his sister. Grandfather was nodding and smiling at the strangers. They reached out their hands to shake his, mounted their horses and rode away.

Grandfather, looking pleased, explained to Young Corn, "Red Beard has come for the last four years. He always stops to say hello and to ask permission for his wagon train to camp down by the eastern springs. He is the only *Americano* wagon master who does that. The others simply camp where they wish as if the land were theirs. To Red Beard I always say welcome. He has invited us to visit the camp a little later when they have settled down."

⌒

Young Corn's spirits rose with anticipation as she helped Little Brother with his melon up the ladder to the terrace just outside her doorway. As she stirred up the cooking fire, her cousin, Crooked Tooth, called over from the next apartment to ask about the strangers. She saw Grandfather down below chatting with a couple of men returning from the fields. She cut up the squash and added pieces of it to the beans simmering in the pot over the fire, gave tired and cranky Little Brother bits of melon to revive him, and settled down to mend a leather carry-bag.

Mother wearily clambered up the ladder. She had spent the day at a nearby ranch in the large weaving room. She worked there with three other pueblo women at the Spanish-style standing looms and at the newfangled wheel that could quickly spin fibers into yarn. Sometimes she wove very fine cloth of cotton or wool that could be decorated for coverings or clothing, but lately she had been making quick-woven material for coarse sacking and carpeting. For every three pieces she wove for the ranch, she could weave one for her own family, which seemed a fair arrangement.

Now she carried over her arm a small gray blanket with a red stripe for Little Brother.

Father was away on some mysterious errand. Young Corn's older brother, Piñon Boy, along with his good friend Apache, was off with the *ciboleros*, hunting buffalo on the plains to the east. When too many of the few remaining men were away from the pueblo, people got nervous. Who would protect them from the occasional raiders who swept through the area? Who would keep some of these new Mexican settlers from stealing whatever they wanted?

Not long ago, Grandfather had found one of the settlers trying to pry the mica window from one of the abandoned houses. He drove off the intruder with a furious barrage of words and curses and threats to summon the government soldiers to punish the man. The Mexican authorities in Santa Fe tried to make sure the settlers respected pueblo rights and property, but the government was far away and overburdened with too many problems to be much help. Little by little, the settlers were setting up farms and ranches around the new little village of San Antonio nearby and along the river, oozing onto pueblo land with their cattle, crops and houses. There simply weren't enough Pecos people to drive them away. It was a constant worry for the elders.

On the other hand, some of the Mexican ranchers, like the ones that employed Mother, treated the Pecos people fairly and respectfully. Piñon Boy and Apache helped with the sheep shearing and herding cattle. They had learned many useful skills from the workers there.

Grandfather sometimes told about the Comanche troubles of the old days, stories he had heard from his father. A resourceful Spanish governor had led a militia army—Grandfather's father had ridden in it—to attack the Comanches on their own ground on the plains. They had killed *Cuerno Verde*, Green Horn, the charismatic chief, who wore a buffalo headdress with the horns painted green, and he brought the rest of them to a peace conference at Pecos Pueblo. Grandfather was a small boy then. He remembered the great tall plains men with their feathers, the shining helmets of the Spanish soldiers, the Governor's beautiful horse, and the fearful excitement as they all gathered at the pueblo.

Though other tribes raided occasionally, the dreaded Comanches did not. New settlers surged into the valley where they had not dared to live earlier, setting up their homesteads wherever the land seemed productive. A new village was growing into a town, San Miguel del Vado, around a convenient river crossing a little way downstream. The tower of the church and some of the homes of the nearby village of Saint Anthony could be seen from the rooftop of the pueblo.

The Pecos people had exchanged one problem for another, the Comanches for the settlers. It was hard to tell which was more devastating. No wonder so many families had moved away!

Young Corn fingered the pendant around her neck. Bits of polished shell and turquoise surrounded the old bone bead. Her grandmother had given it to her before she died, telling her that the ancient bone bead would connect her with the spirits of the ancestors. At first Young Corn had been proud to wear it, but now sometimes she hated it. It seemed to chain her to this sad and dreary place from which she longed to escape. But she still wore it in memory of her grandmother.

⌐

Later, Young Corn joined Grandfather and three others from the pueblo for the walk over to the wagon train. Grandfather's joints hurt him a lot nowadays, and she could tell such a walk, even a relatively short one, was very painful. He never complained, though. She carried the net bag of corn she had gathered earlier, a present for their guests. Grandfather had insisted.

As they neared the camp, they could see huge numbers of oxen and some horses grazing on the meadows. Men on horseback with pistols at their belts watched over them. Then the wagons came into sight. There were seventeen of them drawn up into a huge circle, their white canvas tops gleaming in the late afternoon sunshine. Red Beard came out to welcome them. He and Grandfather sat on a wagon tongue trying to converse, gesturing with their hands, laughing at their clumsy attempts to communicate and at their misunderstandings.

Young Corn looked around the camp. Close up, the wagons looked weary from their long journey across the plains from someplace called Missouri. The canvas tops were stained and dirty, red and blue paint was peeling off the wooden sides, and signs of repairs and patching were visible everywhere. Two men were working on a wheel, heating the iron rim on the coals of a small forge and hammering it back in place. Others were stuffing gobs of grease around the wheel hubs and axles. She already knew that oxcarts needed lots of grease to keep the wheels turning easily.

Several small cooking fires glowed within the circle, and men were bending over them preparing the meals. Some of the fires had iron grills placed over the flames on which huge blue coffee pots were steaming. Copper pots were suspended on hooks over other fires. Beans, like the familiar *frijoles*, were simmering over many of them with onions and bits of bacon making them smell fragrant. Some slabs of beef were sizzling over coals, and some strange kind of bread was baking in frying pans upended in front of the flames. One of the cooks was roasting the corn she had brought, laying the unhusked ears on top of the coals.

She didn't see any women or children, but one of the cooks looked not much older than she was. Some of the men were sitting tiredly on the ground waiting for the food to be ready. One brought out a small instrument that he moved back and forth in front of his mouth while blowing into it. It made a lovely soft sound like wind blowing through the grass, which she gradually realized was a tune.

The young cook poured coffee into a blue cup, spooned in some sugar and offered it to her with a friendly smile. She noticed that Grandfather had a cup also. She tasted it. The coffee was hot and bitter and she didn't like it much, but she drank it anyway to be polite. As she handed the cup back, she nodded her thanks. "Thank you," the young cook coached her, but the sounds wouldn't come right as she tried to repeat them. They both laughed.

Some settlers had come over from nearby ranches to see the wagons. They stood around watching everything. Miguel, a boy she knew slightly, came up beside her. "*¿Cuándo se van? ¿Y a dónde?*" When are you-all going? And where to? he asked.

Going away? Who's going away? When? Where? The question startled her. Did Miguel know something she didn't? She shrugged her shoulders and mumbled, "*¿Quién sabe?*" Who knows?

⤶

Just then, Grandfather and Red Beard beckoned her over to one of the wagons. Red Beard was opening the canvas cover. Young Corn peered in with interest. Boxes, bales and bags filled the large space with a sort of nest among them where a person could sleep in stormy weather.

Red Beard pulled out several long packages. Big rolls of cloth of different colors and designs! He unrolled a length of blue with little red flowers stamped on it. He cut off a large piece with the biggest shears Young Corn had ever seen. He draped it over Young Corn's shoulders and outstretched arms, and with gestures and a big grin indicated that it would make a fine dress for her.

Young Corn was surprised and thrilled. She had never dreamed of having anything so fine. Usually, she wore a loose tunic of coarse wool or soft-tanned buckskin, and for special occasions an old black cotton *manta* attached over one shoulder and tied at the waist with a red sash. She wondered how the little red flowers were stuck right into the cloth itself.

Red Beard was unrolling more cloth and cut off a large piece of yellow with blue designs. "Mama," he announced as he laid it on top of the first. Next, a somewhat shorter piece of bright red with yellow spots. "Papa," and he pointed to his own shirt. "Brother," *hermano,* a green piece that she guessed was for Piñon Boy. And a small piece of pink for "Baby," *chico,* for Little Brother. Young Corn was overwhelmed. But something was missing. She pointed to Grandfather and raised her eyebrows in a question. Red Beard laughed and cut off a large piece of purple and laid it across Grandfather's shoulders. Young Corn hesitated. Did she dare? Hesitantly she requested, "*Amigo? Apache?*" Red Beard laughed some more. "*Amor?* Love? Sweetheart?" and cut off a generous piece of orange, the color of the nearby cliffs.

Red Beard's questioning eyebrows went up, and he made sewing motions with his hands. Young Corn didn't know what he meant. He disappeared in the wagon and rummaged around. Eventually, he emerged with a small leather box fastened with a shiny clasp. He opened it and displayed a rack of shining steel needles and some pins all stuck in some soft fabric and several spools of brightly colored thread. And there was a pair of scissors such as Young Corn had never owned. He gathered up the cloth and folded it into a neat bundle with the sewing kit in the middle and handed it back to her.

Some more rummaging and he brought out for Grandfather a clay pipe with a curved stem and a small sack of fine tobacco. Young Corn knew that Grandfather was delighted only by the sparkle in his eyes. But she managed a timid "Zankoo," as the boy cook had tried to teach her. Red Beard looked puzzled for a moment, then understood and with a broad smile patted her on the head.

As they made their way back to the pueblo in the gathering

darkness, Young Corn asked, "Grandfather, how can we repay those kind *Americanos* for these gifts?"

"We already have," he replied, "by welcoming them to camp on our land. Our feelings are very different with them than with most of the wagon trains that pass by. With this one we'll remember each other always."

The next morning, everybody still at the pueblo went out on rooftops, terraces and rock ledges to watch the wagon train pass. The trail went along the other side of the creek, between the farm fields and the mesa. The heavy wagons lumbered along, hauled by teams of eight or ten oxen, the men walking alongside cracking long whips, shouting at the animals and pushing at the huge wheels when they got stuck. Red Beard led the procession on his horse. As he passed the pueblo, he waved his hat and some of the watching people shouted "Goobye" or "Allo" or Zankoo"—the few *Americano* words they had learned.

⌒

Remembering Miguel's question last evening, Young Corn asked her cousin Crooked Tooth who was standing beside her, "Have you heard anything? Are we moving away soon?"

"The sooner the better," her cousin replied. Young Corn had always looked up to her because she was several years older and always seemed to know everything. "This place is too sad and lonely now. There's nothing here for us any more."

"Where do you think we'll go?"

"Who cares? Any place is better than here."

Young Corn watched the last of the extra animals, oxen, horses and some mules and their herders on horseback disappear in the dust down the trail to Santa Fe.

Santa Fe! Maybe that's where they would go. She had been there many times with her family, on business or pleasure or to visit relatives or friends now living there. No longer did all the people and buildings and narrow streets frighten her.

She would wear a red skirt that swished around her knees when she walked and carry handsome water pots on her head from the fountain. She would paint her face with white flour and smoke large cornhusk *cigarros* and dance at the *fandangos* like the Santa Fe women did. She would go to the market in the main plaza every day and marvel at the many wonderful things for sale or trade there. She would bring to the market the corn and the vegetables her family would cultivate in the large garden sloping down to the river behind the house they would build. Or maybe she would bring herbs gathered in the mountains, or eggs from their chickens, or weavings and embroidery her mother would create. She would finally understand the use of the silver and copper coins she had seen changing hands, and she would add her voice to others trying to attract buyers. She would watch all the people from so many different places and flirt with the handsome horsemen. She would go to mass in the big parochial church there and some of the smaller ones in the city. She would see the governor and his soldiers on parade and listen to the music of the bands. She would be there when the wagon trains arrived and watch them unload marvelous things, and Red Beard would remember her. She would use her Spanish name, Elena, which she had almost forgotten. And there would be no problem finding a handsome husband when she was ready.

Somebody called, and as she turned her head her pendant thumped on her chest. She looked down at the ancient bone bead gleaming in the sun. It seemed to be saying to her, "Don't forget! You are Pecos! Do not lose your heritage as so many have done in Santa Fe."

Young Corn flushed with embarrassment. Somehow, she felt she was betraying her people with this dreaming. Then she was angry at the bead for intruding into the lovely fantasy she was building up. She would have ripped it off and thrown it into the bushes, but suddenly she felt afraid. She went back to her many tasks, part of her mind still speculating about life in Santa Fe and part of it afraid of the possibility.

Later, as Young Corn was coming up from the creek. She recognized two mules laden with large packs standing patiently in the plaza. The Old Mexican Trader had arrived. He stopped often at the pueblo to rest himself and his animals and sometimes stayed for a few days in one of the empty apartments. He and Grandfather had become good friends.

She saw that the two old men were sitting on a mat, their backs against a wall with cups of strong black coffee the trader had brewed in their hands. They were smoking in their pipes some of the fine tobacco Red Beard had given Grandfather. She liked to listen to their conversations, full of bits of news and gossip about people and events throughout the area. She could understand their Spanish quite well. As she passed back and forth on her errands, she recognized that they were remembering the old days when they were young. They were recalling a story she had heard many times about the fiesta in Santa Fe celebrating Mexican independence from Spain. Both men had been there.

"What a lot of excitement," the trader was saying. "I remember when a group of your Pecos people, dressed as bulls and bears, rushed into the plaza and started chasing everybody. They were so realistic that the women screamed and the soldiers reached for their guns. And one of the bears charged up to the general himself and growled at him with his paws raised as if to tear him apart . . ."

". . . and the general screamed and tried to run away like the women did. I was that bear," Grandfather continued. "I was lucky not to have had my head shot off." And both men laughed at the memory.

"Things have changed since then, Amigo," reflected the trader. "Now we are all Mexican instead of Spanish. And because of the new trade laws, we don't have to buy everything through Spain and Mexico and the *Americanos* come in from Missouri bringing good things like this coffee and tobacco. Your people are getting fewer and fewer. How many are there here now? Will you be staying on? For how long?"

By now, Young Corn was openly listening, hoping not to be noticed.

"Who knows, my friend," Grandfather replied. "Our people have lived here forever. The land is sacred to us. The bones of our ancestors are buried here, and their spirits give us strength and courage. Our gods and our hearts will always mingle here, and our prayers are in this place. It will be hard to leave. But we cannot stay. Wherever we go, I'll remember you and hope you will occasionally bring your mules and seek us out."

Young Corn rocked back on her heels. For so long she had longed to leave "this place." She had never realized all it might mean to the elders. "This place" was the heart and soul of her Pecos people! She glanced down at the bone bead on her chest. What was here, really here, that she was so eager to leave behind?

⌇

Later, she helped Mother clean out one of the storerooms. What a lot of trash! Broken baskets, a couple of cracked pots, worn-out sandals, a feather blanket eaten by bugs, tired tools, old corncobs and more. She threw them on the rubbish heap that stretched all along the east side of the pueblo. Over many years—generations—dirt had blown in and grass had grown, making much of the trash heap a gentle slope between the rocky ridge and the meadow. Only the part near the present living area was still used. Young Corn knew that many of her ancestors, and her grandmother, had been buried in the soft earth there. She wondered how many layers of other things, like those she was discarding, might be found by someone digging in the dirt. She stretched her back and wondered when she and Mother would find time to sew the wonderful new cloth that Red Beard had given them. Mother kept saying, "Yes, yes, but first we have to throw out the trash and then grind corn at the *metates* and then . . ." It was just one thing after another.

She looked out over the large open meadow where, according to the elders' stories, great trade fairs had been held in the past. People came from everywhere, near and far, with goods of every sort to trade. The field had been covered with tents, tipis, campfires and horses, dogs and children, people bargaining with each other sharing news and ideas and new things that might make life easier and richer. People were eating and dancing and flirting and having a grand time. It must have been a joyful sight. But nobody came to trade any more. The growing towns farther down the river had become lively trade centers themselves. Even raiding parties from the plains generally left Pecos alone now because there wasn't much left to steal.

⌐

Farther away, along the trail that led to San Miguel del Vado and the several ranches beside the river, she noticed a couple of oxcarts and some heavily laden mules heading for the nearby village of Saint Anthony. This was not unusual. Riders, farm wagons and mule trains often traveled along that way.

But as she watched, three men and two of the mules turned off toward the pueblo. Little Brother, who had followed her, started jumping up and down and squealing with excitement. Piñon Boy and Apache were coming home.

She shouted to Mother, and everybody within earshot dropped whatever they were doing and rushed out to greet them.

The mules were loaded with dried buffalo meat, hides, bones for tools, sinews for cordage, tallow for candles and much more, and an assortment of things traded from the Comanches. What treasures! Quickly, they unloaded the animals, which the third man took back to their nearby ranches. The boys looked strong and healthy, sparkling with vitality, eager to tell their stories. But first, they had to greet the elders and perform certain rituals of return.

Soon, buffalo meat simmered in a huge pot of vegetables and piles of fresh tortillas steamed fragrantly. The few people still left at the pueblo, twenty-five or thirty of them, gathered around the rooftop fireplace to welcome the returning boys.

They had gone out to the plains country with a group of *ciboleros*, buffalo hunters, from San Miguel del Vado and nearby villages. The flat, open country made Piñon Boy nervous so far away from the protecting mountains and mesas and streambeds he was used to. For Apache, this country seemed vaguely familiar. They were both anxious about any hostile tribes they might fight, though they knew the Comanches would not trouble them. The older men with them delighted in teasing the boys, recounting terrible tortures that plains people inflicted on their captives, the narrow escapes they had personally experienced, the dangers that surrounded them on all sides such as prairie fires, deadly thirst, violent storms, hungry wolves. The boys were afraid to go to sleep.

Eventually, they came across a huge herd of buffalo, the biggest and fiercest animals the boys had ever seen. Big, black, hairy creatures with sharp curved horns that could impale a horse or kill a careless rider. Masses of them, stretching as far as the eye could see. They watched in awe as the hunters dashed their horses into the midst of the herd, spearing the animals with their long lances so that they fell dead almost immediately. When the animals stampeded, the ground shook beneath their hooves, trampling any unwary human that got in their way. Four horses were killed and two riders injured. Many of the animals were felled.

The boys were skinners and butchers. With their sharp knives and hatchets they cut up the carcasses, stripped off the hides and rough-cured them. They sliced the meat into thin strips and hung them up to dry before packing them into rawhide bags. It was hard and bloody work. They were given four hides and several bags of meat for their labor.

Once they met some Comanches. One of the men had brought along a couple of bags of "cookies," hard-baked sugar and flour concoctions of which the Comanches were particularly fond. The "cookies" were so hard the Indians had to break them up with their hatchets and soak them awhile in water or hot coffee before they could eat them. They traded a fine rifle, three horses and some beaded moccasins for the privilege.

As they talked about their adventure, Young Corn's eyes scarcely left Apache. Nobody remembered where he came from, whether he had been sold or traded or merely abandoned by a group of visiting Apaches. He was a small boy then and remembered very little about his people. Grandmother had taken him in, and he had grown up alongside Piñon Boy. They were best friends and inseparable companions. The only problem was that Apache, as an outsider, could not participate in the once-rich ceremonial life of the pueblo, the kivas, the dances, the many rituals. This troubled Piñon Boy, but Apache didn't seem to mind. He had grown into an attractive, strong, energetic young man. Young Corn was secretly in love with him, but he was too much like a brother for her to consider him as a possible husband. He was enamored with Crooked Tooth who ignored him.

⌒

Young Corn's mind wandered. She wondered what it might be like to move to San Miguel del Vado. Downriver a ways, it was a settlement growing around a convenient ford across the stream. Many little adobe houses with large gardens and communal pastures dotted the landscape. There was a plaza with a fine little church whose priest sometimes came to Pecos. Two small flourmills ground wheat and corn for nearby farmers and householders. Water channeled from the river turned the heavy stones. The millers, cheerful fat men usually covered with fine white flour dust, poured the whole kernels into one container, and meal or flour of different consistencies would pour into another. No more hours of laboring over the *metates!* How she would appreciate that!

Her *Tía* Rosalia, Mother's youngest sister, lived at San Miguel. Young Corn had visited her on various occasions for several days at a time. She helped out when her babies were born, when there was a special fiesta, or "just because."

Tía Rosalia was married to *Tío* Antonio. He was a *genízaro*, Indian by blood, Spanish/Mexican by upbringing. Like Apache he had little memory of his original people, but the family that had taken him in had cared for him over the years, finally sending him out with two horses, some *pesos* and many useful skills, to live as he liked. An excellent leather worker, he made handsome saddles for ranchers all up and down the valley. He understood animals and sometimes accompanied caravans as a mule driver, loading and caring for the animals assigned to him with great sensitivity and efficiency. He was a fine horseman and one of the best of the *ciboleros*, galloping along with the stampeding herds, thrusting his lance precisely into a vital area that killed quickly and painlessly. H was also full of humor, jokes, songs and stories that delighted his listeners and made him fun to be with. He was the one who had invited Piñon Boy and Apache on the buffalo hunt.

Tía Rosalia tended to him, to the children, to the animals, to the garden, to the church, to the neighbors and to strangers passing by. She was good humored, busy and calm amidst constant turmoil. Young Corn had always enjoyed the time spent with her.

But as she thought about it, she realized that *Tía* Rosalia had forgotten what it was like to be a Pecos. She spoke Spanish constantly, and the Pecos language was unfamiliar to her children. She called Young Corn by her Spanish name, Elena. The life and rituals of the pueblo were not part of her life, and she had not returned to the pueblo for years. She even made fun of Young Corn's habit of honoring the new day, a good meal or special event by scattering a pinch of the corn meal carried in the small pouch attached to her belt. Several Pecos families had moved to San Miguel, but the town was mostly made up of *genízaros* and Mexicans, and there was no Pecos community life that she could see.

Was that where she really wanted to live? She wondered.

⌒

Young Corn spent much of the next day scraping and cleaning the buffalo hides and making sure the slices of meat packed in the rawhide bags had dried hard enough not to spoil. Grandfather and the other elders were spending an unusual amount of time in the kiva, or carrying out carefully-wrapped bundles to someplace outside the pueblo. Mother seemed distracted, puttering about the house and storerooms, brushing off conversation and questions in an unusually abrupt manner. Piñon Boy and Apache were working in the fields, helping others with the harvest and bringing into the pueblo whatever crops were ready. Little Brother wandered around restlessly, getting in everybody's way, fretful at the lack of attention. Something was bound to happen soon, but Young Corn wasn't sure what it might be.

As she worked, she thought about other places they might move to. The Pecos had sometimes been friends with the Taos people up north, but she had never gone that far herself and had no idea of what it might be like there. With the Tewa who occupied several pueblos north of Santa Fe, there lingered a lot of tension and distrust because of earlier conflicts.

Her thoughts kept returning to Cochiti Pueblo, south and west of here on the other side of the Big River. Several Pecos families had moved there, and she had visited them with her own family, riding in the mule cart or running along beside it. The rickety bridge across the river was scary with the brown water rushing below, and it had to be replaced every year after the spring floods. The Cochiti were friendly, and their life and ceremonies were familiar, even though the language they spoke was different from the Pecos. Their extensive farm fields beside the river were well watered. On the pasturelands, cattle and horses grazed. The nearby mountains provided timber and firewood, hunting and sacred sites. So far, Mexican settlers in the area were few.

Some of the men at Cochiti made fine drums, big ones that boomed and smaller ones that "binked" with different pitches. At the feast days, the drums throbbed and the deep voices of the singing men vibrated the air. The numbers of dancers depended on the ceremony or the season. The men were dressed in traditional kilts with foxtails swinging behind, and sometimes they wore animal heads. The women wore black *mantas* and colorful *tablas* on their heads. Shell anklets rattled with each step, and evergreen branches, feathers and turquoise held their own meanings. Every movement was precisely coordinated with the others in true demonstration of community. These dances filled the plaza with ancient spiritual power. It was impressive! She had never experienced anything so powerful.

Maybe Cochiti would be a comfortable place to live, among pueblo people like themselves. Lots of them! Would they go there?

⌒

Later that afternoon, Father returned. Four strange men accompanied him. The language they spoke was very similar to Pecos. Mother explained that they came from Jemez, a pueblo across the far western mountains. They disappeared immediately into the kiva with the elders. Mother and the other women sent food down to them. They were still there in intensive conversation when Young Corn went to sleep that night.

The next morning, the news was spread. The Pecos people would go to Jemez. Immediately. The following day. They had one day to get ready. They would take only what they could carry on their backs.

Mother protested to Grandfather, "We should take all we can. We are proud Pecos people. We can't arrive at Jemez like beggars. We have much to offer that community. We'll take our buffalo hides and dried meat, corn and beans and the seeds of many plants. And our chickens. We'll take our best blankets and a few of our best pots, some necessary tools. Our household goods and sacred objects. We'll take the mule cart and our donkey, as well as ourselves. Father, you can't walk far and you'll need to ride in the mule cart sometimes, and so will Little Brother."

Grandfather shrugged his shoulders and conferred again with the elders. All right, they agreed, but only up to a point.

The day was very busy with everybody sorting and packing what they would take and arguing about limited space in the small cart. What a relief when two more Jemez men arrived with a large wagon pulled by two mules.

The Jemez men helped to organize as much as strangers could and brought in more of the harvest to take along. That, too, caused argument. Why harvest crops they couldn't take with them in the limited space in the wagons and that they couldn't properly process for storage? Yet, they didn't want to leave them for the settlers to steal.

Piñon Boy, Apache and Grandfather drove the small cart over to the old mission church and removed the large picture of Our Lady of the

Angels from its place over the altar. They took it down to the new little church of San Antonio in the nearby village. There they had a long talk with the caretaking *mayordomo* and some of the other parishioners. Yes, they agreed to care for the painting, to hang it in a prominent place in their church, and to celebrate the Pecos feast day every year on the first Sunday in August. They also offered to watch over whatever the Pecos people had to leave behind until they could come back to fetch what they wanted. Grandfather and the boys returned to the pueblo with the loan of another wagon and a team of mules to pull it.

Toward evening, disaster struck. Piñon Boy emerged from the kiva, his face contorted with distress. The Jemez elders had insisted that only "true" Pecos would be welcome. Apache would not be included. His best friend would have to stay behind.

Young Corn felt shattered. She couldn't imagine life without Apache. She loved him like a brother—or more. Would Piñon Boy decide to stay here with him, or would he go along to Jemez with the others? She didn't know anything about Jemez Pueblo and its people. Would they be friendly? Would it be a comfortable place to live? Would she like it there? Shivers of anxiety racked her body, mixed with distress at the loss of her friend Apache. And a generalized rage at the whole situation.

Apache was more philosophical than the rest of the family, though Young Corn could see his jaw muscles twitching strangely. "I'll be all right," he assured them. "I'll stay nearby where I can keep an eye on your—I mean our—old home. Maybe I'll go to San Miguel. I think *Tío* Antonio could use my help there. Or maybe I'll stay at one of the nearby ranches. They are always looking for good workers. I'll go along to see where you'll be living and then bring back the borrowed wagon and team."

⌣

Young Corn couldn't stand it. She fled and ran to a familiar, favorite rock jutting out into the creek. She flung herself down and cried. Too many conflicting emotions! Sadness at leaving the only home she had known and relief that they would be living in a happier place. Fear and uncertainty about the new life and people that would surround them. Sorrow at the loss of Apache and a sneaking desire to stay here with him. Anger at the ties that held her to this place and created this situation

She glared at the bone bead on her chest. "Let me go! Set me free! I don't want to see you any more with your reminders of the Pecos past. I hate you. Stay here where you belong!"

She tore off the pendant, dug a hole in the creek mud with her fingers, and shoved the ancient bone with its accompanying shells and turquoise down as deep as she could. She got up and started back to the pueblo, but something held her back. She opened the little pouch at her belt and took out a pinch of the sacred corn meal, then a handful, and sprinkled it into the fast-filling hole. Then she turned away, wiping tears off her cheeks.

It was a sad night. The wagons were loaded, the animals ready, the packs prepared. But so much had to be left behind, perhaps to be retrieved later, perhaps not. The men were all in the kiva completing prayers or final rituals. Piñon Boy and Apache were together on the stony ridge beyond the pueblo. The women sat on the rooftops huddled in their blankets absorbing the beloved scenery for the last time. The full moon shone a silvery light over everything, outlining the walls of the ancient pueblo, glinting on the water in the creek, creating deep shadows that crawled up along the edge of the mesa. Young Corn sat hunched up, hugging her knees, totally miserable, her eagerness for new places totally forgotten.

Well before dawn, the elders emerged from the kiva. "Time to go!" they announced.

The people shouldered their burdens, laid sleeping children on the overloaded wagons, looked around one last time, and followed the elders out the entryway toward their future.

Young Corn started out with Mother. Suddenly, a stab of pain exploded in her heart. The bone! The Gift from the Ancestors! In her anger she had abandoned it. Now she needed it! How would she know what it meant to be a Pecos in a strange place? What would help her remember her rich heritage? How could she carry the ancestral spirits that would give her strength and courage wherever she went? She had to go back, to find it, to look for it in the mud. She stopped in her tracks.

But Mother grabbed her arm and Crooked Tooth pushed her from behind.

"Come, Daughter. We can't go back now. We must move on. A new life is waiting for us."

And she went.

Part III

Still Here

9. The Bull and Our Lady (1996 AD)

In their new home, the Pecos few became many and over the
years earned the status of an Independent Federally Recognized Tribe
affiliated with Jemez. Each August, two great fiestas involve the Pecos
descendants, their Jemez relatives and friends.

On August 2, the Feast Day at Jemez gathers the whole community
in traditional dances, in feasting and welcoming visiting relatives and
friends from other places. The appearance of the traditional Pecos Bull,
lampooning the Anglo cowboys, brings joy and laughter to all.

And on the first Sunday in August, at Pecos, the picture (now a facsimile)
of Our Lady of the Angels is returned to the ruined mission church by
the congregation of the local Catholic church of San Antonio with an
impressive procession and festive mass, followed by a party in the picnic
area. This keeps the promise made to the Pecos Pueblo people before the
remnant moved away. Many of their descendants return to their ancestral
homeland for the day.

What do these fiestas tell young urban Indians who have lost contact with
their heritage?

10. The Ancestors Return (1999 AD)

The Native American Graves Protection and Repatriation Act
(NAGPRA) that was passed in 1990, mandated that all museums and
universities that receive federal funds should return to appropriate
tribes all human remains and sacred objects as requested.

May 22, 1999, was the day the Pecos ancestors returned home.
The remains of more than 2,000 people excavated between 1915 and 1929
by archaeologist Alfred Kidder were brought back for reburial at Pecos.

This was one of the most significant repatriations
of human remains at that time.

But why were they dug out? Where were they taken?
What happened to them? What's the role of archaeology at the Park?
How does the National Park Service care for this ancient homeland?
In what sense are the Pecos people "still here?"

9

The Bull and Our Lady (1996 AD)

BOOM, BOOM, **BOOM**, Boom, *Boom*, Boom, *Boom* . . . "Hiyah, Hiyah, Hiyah!"

Laura could feel the drums echoing her heartbeat, the deep-voiced chants of the singers vibrating through her spirit. Her bare feet held the rhythm as she danced down the dusty plaza. Like the woman in front of her, like all the women and girls in the line, she lifted her feet just a little, keeping them close to the ground in respect for the greatest of women, Mother Earth.

Father and her older brother Joe danced by with the men in the opposite line. They lifted their knees and stamped their feet vigorously, making the strings of cowrie shells and bells wound around their ankles echo the rhythm.

Up to the brush arbor at one end of the plaza they danced, saluted the pueblo governors and elders sheltered in its shade, turned and danced back slowly to the other end of the plaza. Grandfather was among the singers clustered around the big drums. Laura thought she could distinguish his voice among the others. She couldn't see Mother in the pulsing, weaving blur of color and rhythm and bodies, but other family members and friends lashed across her awareness as they passed each other.

The dance was a prayer, the dancers the prayers. When everything is done right according to ancient tradition, the dance and the dancers and the praying spectators come together in one powerful spiritual force.

The spirits of the earth and sky, of rain and growing things will hear the thanks of the people and grant a good harvest for the well-being of the pueblo.

Though the dance absorbed most of her concentration, little distractions kept breaking in. She saw a tourist with sunburned head thrust his camera at the little girl dancing in front of her while his wife, wearing an identical Hawaiian shirt, squealed, "Isn't she adorable!" Immediately, one of the watching guardians of the dance plucked the camera out of his hand and led the couple away.

Her gaze flicked over some of the younger visitors lining the plaza. Were any of them her cousins from California coming here for the feast days? Had they arrived yet? What would they be like?

In each hand she carried a small evergreen sprig, symbol of life. How many trees in the mountains had provided so much greenery for all of the several hundred dancers? Luckily, they could grow more branches before next year

On the *tablita* attached to her head a cut-out cloud symbol invited rain, and little white feathers waved in the breeze, lifting her prayers upward. He black manta was attached over her right shoulder and tied at the waist with a belt of bright red and green designs that she had woven herself. Her best silver, turquoise and shell jewelry sparkled in the sun.

The men dancers wore white kilts with red and green borders and had fox pelts tied to their woven sashes, the bushy tails drooping and swinging behind. Across their chests that were streaked with orange paint and sweat, cotton straps held jingling shells and little bells. They shook the gourd rattles and green sprigs in their hands in the rhythm of the dance. Most of the things worn and carried in the dances had been handed down through many generations and were cared for like the sacred family treasures they were.

Laura stumbled on an unnoticed stone, dropped her evergreen sprig, and hopped a few steps on one foot while nursing her stubbed toe. Quickly, she was pulled out of line while a *tarboosh*, one of the sacred clowns, retrieved the sprig, checked her foot, and returned her to her place.

"It's okay, Laura, hang in there," he assured her in the Towa language of the Pecos and the Jemez people. She recognized one of her uncles who was disguised by the bright orange paint on his face and stripes around his mostly-bare body, and by the cornhusks attached to his head. She felt relieved because the *tarboosh* often made public ridicule of any dancers who made mistakes.

Finally, the dance was over. The drums stopped and the dancers, more than two hundred of them, filed quietly out of the plaza, up the ladder to a large, square second-story kiva and out the other side. Almost immediately, more drums sounded and another huge group of dancers, with turquoise paint instead of orange, filed into and filled the plaza. They were the winter people who alternated throughout the day with Laura's squash-colored summer people, together calling to the spirits through the power of the dance.

⌒

Laura took her cup of cold Kool Aid over to the folding chairs set up by her family. Grandmother, who hadn't been dancing, was just leaving to tend to her kitchen. For the moment, the three other chairs were unoccupied.

It was good to sit down for a bit, Laura thought. Now she could watch more of the dancing than when she was concentrating in the midst of it. The August day was hot and she was tired. She had spent the last three days helping Grandmother, Mother and Aunt Evelyn prepare food for today's feast, scrubbing, chopping, grinding, measuring, stirring, mixing endless quantities of ingredients. . . . And then there were the long hours of practice and prayer to make sure the dances would go as planned.

All the Turquoise people, like the Squash people before them, filled the plaza, their feet and bodies moving with the rhythm of the drums, their rattles and shells echoing the chants.

There were children, grandparents, and every age in between. Fat people's bellies jiggled and thin ones were flat as boards. Some of them looked strong, others frail. Some had traditional long hair, others curly perms or crew cuts. Some faces were weather-beaten from outdoor work, others with the softer look and stylish glasses of office workers. Some with lots of money who often traveled to New York or Australia or Rome, others subsisting on welfare

Some had earned PhDs, others had barely finished fourth grade. Some were teenagers absorbed in boy/girl relationships, others oldsters who had buried mates and children. Some were struggling to adapt to the demands in the Anglo world, others content to shield themselves within the pueblo cocoon. Some were aware and knowledgeable about their long heritage, others just seeking to find it. What a variety! Laura thought.

Some were mostly Pecos, others mostly Jemez, many were combinations of both, all speaking the same Towa language, coming together as one community to celebrate this annual feast day in traditional ways going back farther in time than anyone could remember. Feuds forgotten, troubles set aside, the scattered returning home, friends invited to share the celebration. Laura's heart swelled with love and caring about the people and place, past and present, all embraced in the power of the moment.

Hundreds of spectators lined the edges of the plaza, the porches of the houses and the flat rooftops. Most were standing uncomfortably in the dusty heat, others had brought folding chairs and umbrellas. They were mostly quiet, respectful, paying attention to the dancers.

⌇

Laura's concentration was interrupted as two young people plopped themselves down in the chairs beside her. The girl was about her age, the boy a bit older. She looked at them, annoyed. Didn't they have any manners? They might have asked if they could sit there

"Laura!" The boy spoke her name. "They told us we'd find you here. We're your cousins from L.A. I'm Kevin, and this is my sister Katie." He grinned and held out his hand.

Laura didn't know what to say for a moment. These cousins looked like *gringos,* not like her people. Pale, suntanned skin, light curly hair, confident outgoing manner, they seemed very strange relatives to her.

But she didn't have time to respond before Katie was talking. "Laura, I'm so glad to meet you! Real Indian relatives! Tell me, what is that thing on your head? What's this dance all about? Why are some people painted orange and some turquoise? Why aren't you wearing shoes? Don't you have any? Have you lived here all your life? Do you speak English? Where do you go to school?"

Such a barrage of questions! Laura had no idea what to say. This cousin made her very nervous. Fortunately, Kevin broke in.

"Shut up, Katie. Look and listen and maybe you'll learn something. Hey, here comes the Pecos bull!"

The strange creature lurched around the corner into the plaza. A large burlap body spotted with white and black circles, its long neck supported a small head topped by a bunch of brilliant parrot feathers, while a tail of knotted rope dangled behind. Only the legs of the man inside were visible as the animal cavorted through the crowd. In front of it pranced a small horse figure wrapped around the body of a "cowboy" dancer, while this "bull" was herded by a group of white-faced "cowboys" urging it along with long whips that kept getting tangled up in the wrong places and lassos that ended up around the necks of dancers or unwary spectators. A couple of drummers were playing military rat-a-tat-tats in competition with the pueblo drums, while a bugle blew discordant sounds drowning out the men singers.

People howled with laughter as the creature wandered among the serious dancers and chased the striped *tarboosh*. It poked its head into the brush shelter, was banged on the nose by the Pecos governor himself, and charged unsuspecting tourists who retreated screeching. Small children howled as the fearsome beast approached, while laughing parents pinned dollar bills to its burlap hide.

"What is <u>that</u>?" asked Katie, astounded.

Laura had found her voice. "It's <u>our Bull</u>, a tradition brought here from our old home. We're making fun of the Spaniards and the Anglos and their cowboys and cattle. It's a special Pecos contribution to this feast day."

"Why does it look so funny? It's not like any bull I ever saw! Where's your brother? Is your mother out there dancing now? Where is Grandmother's house?"

"Slow down, Katie," admonished her brother.

Laura was getting hungry and wanted to escape from so many questions. "I'll take you to Grandmother's house. Plenty of food there. Come on."

She led them along a dirt street to a blue-painted door near the plaza. Grandfather stood in the doorway welcoming new arrivals, chatting with those departing, speaking in Towa, Spanish or English as appropriate.

"How does he know so many languages?" wondered Katie in awe.

"Come in, come in," he welcomed them. "You must be Kevin and Katie. I'm glad you've come. We'll talk more later."

The room was crowded with people. "Just like the circus Volkswagen impossibly filled with clowns," joked Kevin. Some were sitting on couches in the living room watching TV while waiting for their turn to eat. Others were standing and chatting with long-lost friends or getting acquainted with strangers. Anglos, Hispanos, Indians, even a black family milling around together.

Along the walls were cabinets and shelves displaying pottery, jewelry, beaded moccasins, school awards, while above them hung family photographs, blankets and fancy shawls and beautiful baskets.

And on the long dining room table, surrounded by guests sitting on folding chairs, the great feast was spread. Big bowls of red or green chile, posole, sliced turkey, fried chicken, salads of all kinds, potatoes, Spanish rice, corn, squash, refried beans, bread pudding, pies, Jell-O with tiny marshmallows, horno bread, cookies, tortillas, guacamole, a huge chocolate layer cake, cans of soft drinks, pitchers of iced tea and Kool Aid. Kevin and Katie were amazed.

Laura could see how they stared and heard Kevin whisper under his breath, "Lo, the poor Indian!"

Grandmother, Mother and Aunt Evelyn were running back and forth, refilling serving bowls from the huge containers in the kitchen, bringing in clean dishes, cleaning up any spills, explaining the chile and recipes to Anglo visitors, chatting with guests from far away and friends from nearby towns. As soon as one person finished eating and left the table, clean plates were set out and someone else sat down to eat and joined the conversations around the table. The bustle somehow seemed both relaxed and efficient.

The kitchen, too, was crowded. Huge kettles steamed on the stove, large bowls and platters held additional food, and the sink was piled high with dirty dishes. One chair and a small corner of the table were reserved for Grandfather. Father, still in his dance kilt, leaned against a wall with a bowl of chile and a hunk of horno bread in his hands. Brother Joe was sitting on the back step with a tortilla piled high with an elaborate combination of foods. Kevin took the bowl of chile Grandmother thrust into his hands and commented on how much there was to eat.

Father laughed, "Oh, pueblo women spend half their lives preparing food." This was obviously part of an ongoing family joke.

"And you men spend half your lives eating it while we clean up," grinned Mother. "Food is important, Kevin, and we enjoy preparing it because we women all work together—and (to Father) your ears would burn if you knew what we say about you men."

Aunt Evelyn came in from the dining room to refill a salad bowl and added, "But that's not all we women do. We're teachers and potters and computer programmers and nurses and social workers as well as wives and mothers and cooks."

"That's amazing!" commented Kevin. "But why do you serve so much food to all those people when so many of them aren't even Indian?"

Mother explained, "Last year, we fed over two hundred! We're thankful for what we have and we show our thanks by sharing it with others. It's a good time to welcome friends and relatives to our home."

"With all those tourists? You can't afford that! Why don't you charge them something, or leave a basket for donations by the door?"

Someone said something in Towa and everybody started to laugh.

"Father said you sound like a tourist yourself," explained Laura. "Just leave us a bunch of money when you're done. And anyway, these white people aren't tourists. They're friends we work with, go to school with, or we have known for a long time. We always invite them to spend the day with us."

Through the doorway, Joe added, "Sure we make fun of white people. Some of them are pretty funny, but so are we. Have you watched any of our professional Indians who strut around trying to impress the tourists? We call them 'Geronimos.' Some visitors who don't know any better make us laugh, like that fat man who started to climb into the kiva this morning and almost fell off the ladder when the *tarboosh* appeared in his paint and feathers to chase him away. And that obnoxious woman in high heels and tons of silver and turquoise jewelry who stood in front of the elders so they couldn't see the dancing. Or that kid who tried to swipe a dropped earring thinking nobody would notice, and his expression when one of the guardians of the dance caught him. Yeah, there's plenty to laugh at."

Aunt Evelyn popped in again from the dining room and interjected,

"Hey, Joe, we need those people, too. Their cold cash is better than the beads and trinkets and firewater they gave us in the old days. We surely appreciate refrigerators and cars and electricity and microwaves and Kentucky Fried Chicken and ice cream. As for TV—that's questionable."

"Well, what do they get from us?" inquired Kevin.

"Ignorant savages to make John Wayne famous," proclaimed a deep voice, and as Grandfather came into the kitchen everybody laughed.

Kevin went outside to sit with his cousin Joe on the back stoop, and soon Laura could see them deep in animated conversation. Katie hadn't said anything for a long time. She was sucking air into her chile-burned mouth. "How can you eat that fiery stuff," she moaned. "You-all aren't at all like I expected."

"What did you expect?" asked Laura. "Movie Indians? We have some of those around here, too." She wrapped a big apron around her dance dress and tossed Katie a dishtowel. Her voice deepened comically. "Ugh. Squaw gottum plenty work. Heap lotta dishes. Paleface girl help." She plunged her hands into the hot dishwater and together they tackled the dirty dishes.

⌐

The sound of drums called them out for the afternoon dancing. First the Squash people, including Laura and her family, then the Turquoise.

The sun was low when the drums led the last dancers away from the plaza. The side-street vendors had packed up their crafts and cheap plastic gimmicks and snack foods and departed. The pueblo traffic directors had waved off the last of the visitors. The final ceremonies were completed. And everybody, exhausted but exhilarated, straggled back to their homes.

⌐

Eventually, Laura's family gathered again at Grandmother's house. There was still some food left over. Everybody sat around the long table, filling and refilling their plates, relaxed and conversational. Much of the talk revolved around the events of the day, the powerful moments, the funny incidents, the little happenings they had seen. Laura noticed that

Katie had become much quieter as if she were listening, observing and thinking more about all she was experiencing. Her irritation with her talkative cousin changed to curiosity and compassion. After all, this was a wholly new experience for her. And now there was a chance to listen to her and Kevin's stories.

Kevin began. "My grandparents were born here at Jemez, although Dad and some of their ancestors came from Pecos."

"Yes," said Grandfather. "Your grandfather was my brother. Your grandmother also had Pecos blood. She was a Toya, descended from Juan Antonio Toya who had led the last survivors here from Pecos Pueblo. Right after they married, your grandparents went off to apply for the Relocation Program."

"Relocation Program? What's that?" asked Laura.

"In the 1950s when your grandparents and I were young, the U.S. government, with help from some of the Indians themselves, started the program. They wanted to relocate Indians from all over the country to some of the big cities. They believed that if Indians were taken away from their reservations and pueblos they would have more opportunity for education and employment. They would become more like white Americans.

"All we had to do was apply. It was a simple thing to do, they said. Then, if you were accepted, you went by bus to the city of your choice where the government helped you find a job and a place to live. The intention was good, because life was especially difficult for Indians at that time, but it didn't work out as anticipated."

"Yeah," said Kevin. "My grampa used to talk about how they saw a paper with a picture on it. It showed an Indian man dressed in a fancy suit and tie standing by a pretty house with white shutters on the windows and flowers in the yard. The Indian man and his family were all smiling. They made you believe that this would happen to you if you signed up for the program.

"Well, when Grampa and Grama got to L.A., it was not like that at all. The government did pay for the bus trip and their first month's rent, but it was a one-room apartment in a terrible section of the city that the white people called the Indian ghetto.

"Grampa got a job, but that was terrible too. He worked in a big, dirty factory where he never got to breathe fresh air or to see the sun. Grama said that's why he died so young."

Grandfather added, "After he died, your grandmother told me many stories about those early times. She said that living there almost killed her. No matter where they were or what they were doing, there was always a big clock telling them they were supposed to be somewhere else. Anglo time made no sense to them and they couldn't read the clocks anyway. Of all the gadgets, telephones were particularly terrifying! They always got lost on the bus. And the elevators were the worst. The little door opened and they had to crowd in with all those strangers, and when the door opened itself they were pushed out into a different place. They were shy and didn't speak English enough to be able to ask for help. It must have been difficult for them."

Kevin continued, "I guess a lot of Indians went back home."

Grandfather agreed. "Almost all the people from Jemez came back."

"But some had too much pride or not enough money for the bus," continued Kevin. "They wore shabby clothes, didn't have enough to eat and didn't know how to find assistance. Those who would have been warriors in the old days spent their time fighting rats and cockroaches and racism.

"Anyway, Grama and Grampa stayed and had a child, my mother. She went to school there, did well and got a job. That's where she met Dad. He's an Anglo. That's why Katie and I don't look very Indian. Dad went to college, got a good job and brought Grama to live with them. Eventually, we moved to a really nice neighborhood where we now live."

Katie interrupted, "Our house is just a block from the movies. My friends and I go every week. And on Saturdays we ride the bus to the big shopping mall. That's where I got these cool jeans and Nikes." She looked down at her feet.

Laura wondered what it would be like to be able to go to the movies or the malls whenever you wanted, and had the money. She only got to do that when Mother or friends went to Albuquerque or Santa Fe, which wasn't very often.

"Do you live near the ocean?" she asked. "I've never seen it, nor gone to a beach . . ."

Joe interrupted, "Kevin tells me he plans to study marine biology and spend his life in boats and along the shore trying to save the sea creatures from human-caused destruction. A good thing to do!"

Kevin added, "And Joe wants to study environmental science so he can do the same thing around here. As cousins, we're more related than we thought."

"What's it like, growing up as Indians in L.A.?" asked Laura.

Kevin laughed, "People look at us and don't believe our Indian ancestry. Both the white people we know and the few real Indians in our schools and neighborhoods laugh at us and call us 'Wannabes.' It's insulting! Some of our best friends are Orientals and Blacks who seem to understand us better."

"Well, how do you learn about your Indian heritage?" continued Laura.

"Mother tries to tell us all she can. We watch TV documentaries and read books out of the library. But we don't know much, and that's why we're here. What's it like for you, Joe and Laura, growing up in this ancient pueblo community?"

"Confusing!" reported Joe. "Here at home we have one set of values and ways of behavior, and out there in the Anglo world we have to deal with totally different perspectives. Often they conflict. It's like two separate worlds, and we have to learn how to adapt to each without betraying our people or ourselves."

"Some people manage it very successfully," commented Father. "They do well in the outside world without losing their roots. Some return to the pueblo with their skills to help the people here. For others, it's very difficult and they either abandon their Indian background—as much as the Anglo world will let them—or they retreat back here to the safety of the pueblo. Unfortunately, some just can't cope and take to drugs and alcohol and end up in jail, or dead. But the arts have been a good bridge. Your Aunt Evelyn, for instance, is totally Pecos and Jemez. Her beautiful pottery brings good prices, and she is comfortable dealing with everybody under the sun all over the United States."

"I go to the Santa Fe Indian School," continued Joe. "We have mostly Indian teachers and students from all of the New Mexican pueblos, as well as a few Navajos and Apaches. It helps us figure out who we are and gives us the strength to face the future in the outside world. I play basketball and run cross country with their Braves athletic team."

"I'm going there too," added Laura. "I'm a 'Lady Brave.' Doesn't that sound silly?"

"Katie, what do you want to study? What do you want to do with your life?" Mother asked.

Katie hesitated, "I used to want to just work at the mall, with so many shops and wonderful things for sale. But now I wonder if I should think more about merchandizing or advertising, helping Indian people sell their products."

"What about you, Laura?" asked Kevin.

Laura opened her mouth and a totally surprising idea popped out. "I want to be a National Park Ranger!"

"A WHAT?" several voices exclaimed in astonishment.

"Yes, a Park Ranger. Then I can help people like Kevin and Katie learn more about their own heritage, protect the old homelands at places like Pecos, look after the environment like Kevin and Joe, and so much more . . ." She hadn't thought about it before, but the more she considered the possibility, the more attractive it seemed.

"Well, we go to Pecos tomorrow," Father reminded. "You can practice on all of us there."

⌒

"Okay, Ranger Laura. What's there at Pecos and why are we going there today? Can you enlighten your big-city relatives from far away?" This was Kevin talking as they settled down in the car for the long drive.

He sounded as if he was making fun of her, and Laura felt distinctly uncomfortable. Father and Mother and Joe seemed to hold their breaths wondering what she would say. Laura wondered, too. But Katie squeezed her hand in a comforting way, and Laura glanced at her in appreciation.

"Well," Laura began hesitantly, "yesterday was the traditional Jemez feast day of Santiago, and today, all of us who can go back to our ancient home will celebrate the Pecos feast day of Our Lady of the Angels. It's a beautiful place with a lot of meaning for us Pecos. The old mission church is still there, even though it's in ruins. The people from the Pecos village church of Saint Anthony bring back our painting of Our Lady of the Angels, our patron saint, and hang it over the altar as they promised to do when our ancestors left. We celebrate a special mass, and it's a joyful time."

"Will there be dancing?" asked Katie.

"No," filled in Joe. "This is more of the Spanish Catholic part of our heritage. Guitars instead of drums. The local village people will be sending up prayers on our behalf. We're kind of a mixed-up people, somehow combining both Christian and Indian beliefs."

"How come if so few people were left to migrate to Jemez there are so many of you now? It's pretty confusing trying to sort out the Pecos-Jemez connections." Kevin was puzzling over this.

Mother laughed, "When our scattered Pecos people saw how the Jemez had welcomed our pitiful few, some of them came to join us there. Some of our women married Jemez men, and nature took its course. There are enough of us now to be recognized by the U.S. government as a separate tribe affiliated with Jemez. The second lieutenant governor of Jemez is always the Pecos governor."

"Father was that governor last year," commented Laura.

"Wow!" exclaimed Kevin. "What was it like?"

"Educational!" grunted Father as he steered the car around a huge semi.

⌐

The massive red walls of the old church gleamed in the sun as people gathered in the nearby parking lot. They were dressed in their best clothes:

suits and ties for some, bright shirts, colorful skirts or pretty dresses on others. Grandmother wore a fringed Spanish shawl embroidered with brilliant flowers over her blue dress. Little ribbons fluttered on Grandfather's multicolored shirt when he moved. There were old-style lace mantillas covering the heads of elderly Hispanic ladies, cowboy hats, colored head bands, shiny high-heeled boots, well tanned moccasins.

But Katie was staring at the church. "Why is it such a wreck?" she wailed plaintively. "Why don't people build up the walls and put on a new roof?"

Laura didn't know how to respond, but just then Grandfather called to them, in Towa, to get ready for the procession.

Two boys in red robes bearing tall candles followed a white-robed man carrying a large cross. The priest swung a container of incense, its fragrant smoke perfuming the air. Two men playing guitars and one with an accordion led the choir, the singers repeating a refrain in Spanish that everybody could join. Others carried banners and bunches of flowers, and two strong men lugged the famous picture of Our Lady of the Angels. The procession was followed by hundreds of people and made its way into the ruined church. The men carefully hung the picture on the spike embedded in the wall above the flower-bedecked altar at the top of the steps. The people sat down on the folding chairs that filled the open space, while the Pecos descendants, including Laura and her family, were escorted to the front rows. Some tourists stared politely, while park rangers in their distinctive flat-brimmed hats and their volunteer helpers watched over the scene.

The mass began. Hymns, mostly in Spanish, psalms, chants, prayers, Bible readings, a brief homily by the priest. The inevitable collection. The dramatic communion in which the priest held up "the body of Christ" and invited all present to partake of the blessed wafers. The solemn lines of people moving up and back, some with heads bowed in prayer, some weeping with emotion, some with radiant faces. Then speeches, by the Pecos elders, the Park superintendent, the mayor of the village. A final blessing and more hymns as the procession and the people filed out of the church.

Laura was moved almost to tears and noticed that Katie had been sitting rapt, motionless most of the time. What was she thinking? she wondered.

Grandfather was the star of the show. His long prayer in Towa had entranced people and many gathered around to shake his hand or take his picture. His handsome, wrinkled face was wreathed in smiles, and his colored ribbon shirt and striped headband stood out dramatically against the red of the old adobe walls.

◠

Slowly, the crowd moved over to the nearby picnic area. Some of the Hispanic women had spent the morning baking hundreds of sweet rolls and cookies in the old, round-topped *horno* there. There were buckets of lemonade and containers of hot coffee to go with them. Everybody milled around eating, visiting, talking, greeting each other, catching up with news of families and friends. The guitars and accordion were still playing off to one side, with people wandering over to request a tune or to join in a song. It was like a big neighborhood party.

⌒

Katie poked Laura's arm, "Where did all the people live? I don't see any houses."

"Over there," Laura gestured with her chin toward a large, grass-covered mound a short distance from the church.

"Come on," invited Joe. "Let's go over there."

As they walked along the paved path toward the grassy humps, Katie looked utterly distressed. "There's nothing here," she wailed. "Just weeds and rattlesnakes!"

But Kevin was excited. "I took a course in archaeology at school. These mounds must be full of information!"

He and Joe walked along ahead, studying the bits of rock wall still standing, the contours of the land, and the fragments of broken pottery scattered among the weeds.

Surrounded by the humps of the main plaza, Katie wailed again, "What happened to this place? This doesn't feel like anybody's home!"

Joe grinned at her, "Ever hear of recycling? When buildings are abandoned, they fall down. People come and take away old pots and doorways and roof beams and whatever they can use. Then the dirt sifts in, and the archaeologists arrive."

"And the park rangers try to help people understand what was here and how the people lived," added Laura.

"And they put up pictures and signs like this one," remarked Kevin, moving over to look at a metal signboard that showed what that corner of the plaza might have looked like.

"There's a short film down in the Visitor Center that might help you understand what happened here." Laura was trying to be ranger-helpful.

"And a dandy little museum showing all sorts of things the archaeologists found here," Joe added for Kevin's benefit. "We'll stop in the kiva along the way. It was restored by the Park Service and is probably the only one you Californians will be invited into."

By the time they got back to the picnic area, Katie had cheered up and Kevin was spouting with excitement about the things he had been seeing. Most of the people had left by now. Mother and Grandmother had gone back to Jemez with Aunt Evelyn and her husband. Grandfather wanted to stay a little longer.

Laura decided to stay with him.

"We'll take these city folks to Adelo's Country Store in the village and show them what a 'mall' looks like around here, and then we'll let them dabble their toes in the Pecos River upstream a ways. We'll come back for you later," suggested Father, and he went off with Joe and the cousins.

〜

Laura followed Grandfather over to the ancient plaza and joined him sitting on the top steps of the highpoint at the north end of the walls. They could see in all directions. The light and the landscape looked magnificent: the mountains to the north, the distant Pecos River to the east, the creek valley below the mesa to the west and the line of orange cliffs leading out to the plains country to the south and east. Surely it was a very special place! A few late tourists wandered past, their noses in their trail guides. They glanced curiously at the old man and the girl sitting there and ambled on along the path.

Grandfather pulled out his pipe, tamped it full of tobacco, lit it and ceremoniously blew smoke in the four directions, to the sky and to the earth.

"Grandfather, why are you doing that? You know you're not supposed to smoke in the park."

"Laura, we ancient ones have been offering smoke to the spirits and enjoying it ourselves since time began. We're not going to stop now, especially since it helps us communicate with the Old Ones. Why don't you go down by the creek near that big cottonwood and see if you can find any corn plants. And remember, stay on the paved trail."

He winked at her and she grinned back. There was no paved trail down to the creek. Several signs along the way told visitors to stay on the trail, and she felt daring.

By the little shelter overlooking the creek valley, she slid down the slope and began to walk toward the most conspicuous cottonwood she could see. Tall weeds grew all around her. She hoped the rattlesnakes wouldn't bite her. What did Grandfather mean about corn plants? There was nothing like that around here, just brush and weeds.

Then she saw them. Half a dozen stalks with yellow tassels protruding from the young ears. How did they get here? Were they leftover from ancient times? She pulled the weeds away from their stalks and noticed that the ground here near the creek was damp enough to sustain them. They looked strong and beautiful, and she started to sing one of the Corn Dance songs to them.

She continued the short distance to the creek. Not much water was in it at the moment. She plopped herself down on a ledge of rock a couple of feet higher than the creek bed. It seemed like a natural place to sit, and she wondered how many of her ancestors had rested on this rock. She stayed very quiet, listening for the ancient spirits, voices from the past, but all she heard was the rippling of the water, the sound of the breeze in the trees and the insects in the grass.

Little pebbles were piled against the upstream side of the rock, probably left here by the spring runoff. She picked up one, and then others, and tossed them into the stream. They made satisfying little splashes.

Her fingers touched something that was half-embedded in the mud. It shone white. Curious, she dug it out. It was sort of flat and round with a hole in the middle from which a bit of rotten cord dangled. Her searching fingers probed the dirt, and one by one she retrieved four pieces of turquoise and a broken shell, each with a hole drilled through the middle. Must have been somebody's necklace, she thought, and put the pieces in the pocket of her dress.

She heard a voice calling her name and started back up the ridge. As she passed the corn plants, she greeted them politely in Towa, and they seemed to nod back.

Grandfather was waiting for her at the overlook shelter. "Did you find the corn plants?" he inquired.

"Yes, six of them. They look healthy. But how did they get there? Did the rangers plant them and then not take care of them?"

Grandfather grinned mysteriously. He thrust his hand into his pocket and brought out a few kernels of corn—yellow, blue, red. He winked at her and remarked, "It's a great mystery how corn plants keep appearing here when nobody plants them. Corn plants like these are the life of your ancestors and the life of your children. As long as corn is here, so are we, Cicuye/Pecos people. If you take the time to listen and pay attention, these plants can teach you great wisdom."

"Look what I found, Grandfather, by that big rock beside the creek." Laura took out the round bead and the bits of turquoise and shell. The old man examined them carefully, turning them over and over in his fingers.

"There's an old story in our family," he mused. "When my great grandmother left with the others, she buried a special bone bead down by the creek. She called it a gift from the ancestors. She never could find it again, though she searched for it the few times she returned in later years. I wonder if this is it."

Laura felt excited. "Grandfather, can I have it? Can I be the keeper of the gift of the ancestors? I would take good care of it. And after all, I'm the one who found it."

Grandfather was silent for a long while, still turning the bone bead over and over, pondering what to do with it. At last, he said, "This bead belongs to all of our people, and it belongs here in our ancestral home. I think I'll give it to the Park for the moment, to look after on our behalf. A ranger walked by a couple of minutes ago. I'll ask him to make sure it gets to the right Park staffers who would care for it." He got up and walked away, looking for the ranger.

Laura lingered a few minutes longer. The sun was sinking toward the western mesa beyond the creek. The tiny stream began to glow gold, and the glow was picked up by the edges of the corn plants. Now that she knew where to look for them, she could make them out quite clearly.

The corn plants seemed to wave at her. She smiled and saluted them in Towa, "Hey there, Ancestors!" And more than ever she felt at home.

10

The Ancestors Return (May 22, 1999)

Betsy was tired. She nestled on the grass beside Mother. Baby Brother was asleep on a beach towel close by. She rubbed her aching feet and wondered if the blister on her heel would get infected.

Mother must be even more tired. She had lugged Baby Brother most of the way along the old roads and trails over the mountains. They said it was about eighty miles from Jemez to Pecos, three long days of steady walking.

Betsy had protested. It was too far. Three days of nothing but walking didn't make sense. Why couldn't she ride in a car? But Mother hadn't given her a choice.

"You are Pecos and you are Jemez and you are stronger than you know. You are going to walk with me and with the others. We'll honor our ancestors who fled from their homeland to live here with their Jemez relatives in 1838. We'll be retracing the trails they used. We'll be there to welcome the other ancestors returning from the east. We are going back home, to Pecos. This is important, for you, for us, for our people, for our ancestors, for those who will come after us. Here's your pack. Make sure your water bottle is full."

Betsy was tired, but it was a good tired. Yes, she had walked all the way, keeping up with Mother and hundreds of others without complaint. Much of the walk was fun, with all those people from her pueblo, some young, some old and everything in between. They helped each other along, rested under trees, sweated in the sunshine, cooled their feet in little streams, teased and cheered each other when tired or discouraged.

And much of it was hard. They struggled along rough, uphill slopes, endured midday heat and dust, ran out of food and water, and sometimes felt so tired that another step seemed impossible. And that was when Betsy reached out to clasp the hands reaching out to help her, and in turn reached out her hands to help others.

At overnight stops at Cochiti Pueblo and at the Santa Fe Indian School, hot food and mats on the gym floors awaited. She slept like the dead until Mother shook her awake at dawn. How she resisted, begging in vain for "only another hour of sleep!"

Brother Sam had been walking with some of his friends. She had hardly seen him, except once when he had helped her over a fallen log and again when he appeared briefly to tease and taunt her. "Brothers," she had groaned, "are they all like that?"

And she had arrived! Mother was right. She was stronger than she knew.

⤳

This morning, in the gray dawn, they reached the entrance to the Park. Besides the walkers, many other people coming from Jemez in cars and trucks and vans joined them. Father and Grandfather were among them: they had been helping organize the events of the day. Together they waited. And waited. Uniformed Park Rangers slowed down passing cars and helped drivers find places to park. Mother had changed from her jeans and hiking boots to her favorite dress and high moccasins. Betsy had put on her new broomstick skirt and her turquoise necklace over a clean white blouse. And they waited with everybody else in silence.

At last, in the early morning light, appeared the headlights of a huge, gray panel truck. The Ancestors! An honor guard of Jemez Pueblo Police and the National Park Service had escorted them all across the country.

The Pecos elders welcomed the Ancestors with long prayers in Towa and the scattering of sacred corn meal. Dressed in white trousers, colorful ribbon shirts, turquoise and silver jewelry and headbands, they led the way into the Park. The truck was surrounded and followed by a river of people. Some of them cried, some looked exuberant. Someone made a joke. It sounded like Sam, Betsy thought, but the people nearby hushed him.

"The remains of more than two thousand Pecos ancestors are in that truck!" they whispered. *"How could they all fit in? Why had they been taken away so long ago? What happened to them in the east, at Harvard University? How did it happen that they are coming home? Now is the time to welcome them and to celebrate their homecoming!"*

NAGPRA! Betsy had heard Grandfather, Father and Mother and other older people talking about it for a long time. But the word sounded like just a jumble of letters to her. It seemed to mean that a new law insisted that universities and museums all across the country had to return to the tribes that wanted them the remains of ancestors and sacred objects dug up years ago. The meetings, consultations, planning and trips back and forth between Jemez and Massachusetts and the Pecos National Historical Park went on and on. They seemed endless, and sometimes everybody involved despaired of any positive results. But now, today, the Ancestors had finally arrived!

Betsy, her mother and hundreds of people followed the truck a long way back into the Park, to an area that could be protected from vandals and curious sightseers. But only the Pecos descendants were allowed at the burial ceremony itself.

The Park workers had dug a long trench into the earth. The back of the truck was opened up. After more long prayers of welcome, Pecos men carried out the ancestral remains and laid them gently into the trench. Father was helping organize the ceremony. A drum thumped softly from somewhere nearby while the elders were blessing each burial. The watching people were silently offering their individual prayers. Betsy was surprised to see tears running down Mother's cheeks. What a lot of Ancestors were coming home!

Betsy knew that her brother Sam was angry. He had hoped to help with the actual burial, but he wasn't one of the ones chosen. His bad mood showed in his expression and his attitude. She felt sorry because she realized how much he cared.

⌐

At last it was done. The sun was shining brightly and the people moved over to the picnic area near the Park Headquarters. A platform had been set up in the parking lot for the speakers with folding chairs for all the dignitaries.

The Pecos/Jemez people were joined by many more and sat around the platform on folding chairs, on picnic tables and benches, on blankets on the ground, on the grass. They were shaded by big hats, by the trees, by big umbrellas. Betsy was looking at this colorful crowd with their festive dresses and ribbon shirts. These were her people, and she felt happy to be with them, even though she felt tired.

This was the first time Betsy had sat down in hours. She didn't think she could ever get up again. But Mother pulled her to her feet to join other walkers in front of the platform for a special honor song offered by the Jemez Drum Group. It made Betsy feel that she had done something really important.

The speakers went on and on. How they could talk! The Governor of New Mexico, a representative from the President of the United States himself, the Governors and Elders from both the Pecos and Jemez lineages, delegates from other tribes and pueblos, some from far away. Other officials from Washington and Santa Fe, museum directors from the east, people who had worked hard to make NAGPRA a reality. This was its biggest and most significant repatriation to date. A whole array of photographers was busy with cameras. One of them, Betsy had been told, was from the *National Geographic*, a magazine Betsy often read at school. Grandfather was sitting among the dignitaries. He offered a prayer in Towa that was mercifully short.

Mother was sitting up straight, alert and listening to every word with interest. But for Betsy, the words just droned on and on. Would they never finish? She could smell the food being set out at the serving area near the *hornos* and realized that she was very hungry. Her aunts and many of the other women had been preparing the feast for many days.

When the final speaker was just concluding his remarks, VARRRROM! A huge roll of thunder split the clear sky. People looked up, startled. Immediately, a small whirlwind came out of nowhere, flinging clouds of dust and grit all around the parking area. People hunched their shoulders and covered their faces with their hands. Then all was quiet. The people relaxed, smiled, nudged their neighbors, reminding each other, this is the sign the elders had predicted. The Ancestors were happy to be back home again. They are saying Thank You! Mother glanced at Betsy and gave her a big hug.

The hundreds of people stood up, stretched, moved around talking with each other. Betsy could hear bits of conversation. "Powerful moment" . . . "what timing!" . . . "I get the shivers" . . . "the ancestors have spoken" . . . "now we're all together again."

How could so many people be fed? Betsy wondered. The servers would be ready pretty soon.

Betsy spied Grandfather approaching through the crowd. He looked fine in his brightly colored ribbon shirt, moccasins and red headband. His brown wrinkly face was wreathed in smiles, and his turquoise and silver jewelry sparkled in the sun. He stopped to speak with a man in a Park Ranger uniform, a "Flat Hat," and led him over to Mother and Betsy. Brother Sam joined them. Father was still busy elsewhere.

"This is the Park Superintendent," Grandfather explained. "He has been a good friend and very helpful as we planned this special day." The Superintendent shook hands with each person in turn as he was introduced. He was a small, trim man with tan skin, a dark mustache and warm friendly eyes. He stood straight and looked like a leader. Betsy felt comfortable with him but ducked her head, feeling shy. She didn't know what to say to him.

Sam had no such problem. Betsy could see he was still angry. "This is our home, our land," he challenged. "When are you going to give it back to us?"

Grandfather spoke rapidly to Sam in Towa, telling him to mind his manners. Mother was appalled at Sam's rudeness and tried to apologize explaining, "Sam hasn't decided what kind of Indian he wants to be."

This puzzled Betsy. How could Sam be anything other than Pecos/Jemez, just as she was.

The Superintendent was not upset. He turned to Sam. "It's tough for most young people nowadays, trying to figure out who and what they want to be. It gets complicated for all of us, whoever we are.

"But Sam, as for your question. There are no plans at present to give the land back to your people. However, our relationship with the Pecos elders is strong. They spend a lot of time here and we work with them in as many ways as we can. This repatriation of the ancestors is one example. Teachers, artists, archaeologists and many others come here frequently and are always welcome. I expect you yourself came with a school group for a very special tour, perhaps several times, and that you looked at our interpretive film and the museum in the Visitor Center. You probably know a good deal about what we do here."

Sam sat on the ground, head down, shoulders hunched, as if in disgrace at his rudeness. But Betsy could tell he was listening.

"Our job with the National Park Service here is to preserve, protect and present all the elements of this park for all the people. That means we care for the many archaeological sites we keep finding in the back country, for the remains of the Santa Fe Trail and a couple of trading posts, for the Civil War Battlefield—a big one!—and for the ranch that involved cattle, dudes and celebrities. And of course, there's the landscape and natural environment.

"What do you have to protect all this old stuff from?" Sam looked up. He was curious.

"Fire, for one thing," continued the Superintendent, "erosion, decay, deterioration of walls and old buildings. Vandals and pot hunters. Invasive plants that threaten to obliterate the ruins. Trespassers and hostile people who want to damage or destroy places under our care. Greedy developers who buy up land for condo communities. You'd be surprised at the threats we face every day.

"And above all, we try to educate our visitors, interpret the lives and times of past inhabitants, to present our tons of material in ways that can be easily understood. Look at our museum and realize that each item on display is only a sampling and simplification of so much more.

"Sam, when you go up onto the high point of the pueblo ruins, everything you can see in all directions, and a lot more besides, was once part of the Pecos territory. Much of that, including the village, is now privately owned and not available to us. Of course, the ruins of pueblo and church are central to everything else here, and so are a lot of the other things."

"Are you still digging up our ancestors?" Sam's question no longer oozed hostile challenge.

The Superintendent laughed, "No, Sam. That was a different era. Now we have a deep respect for the ancestral remains buried here. There are still thousands of them in the midden and under the house blocks. They will not be disturbed.

"Tell you what, Sam. When the dust dies down a bit and we've caught our breath after today, why don't you come and spend a day with me. Let me show you what we do here, how we are caring for your homeland, and how we struggle with unexpected problems and too much bureaucracy."

Sam said nothing, but from the glint in his eyes and the hint of a smile, Betsy was sure he was delighted at the invitation. Why just Sam? In a tiny, shy voice she asked, "Me too?"

The Superintendent smiled at her and patted her shoulder. "Yes, Betsy. You too!"

⌒

The feast was ready and people were forming long lines to be served. It would take a long time, Betsy realized. Her stomach was growling.

One of her aunts beckoned her over to a side table. "Take this to your grandfather," she said, handing her a plastic plate loaded with food and a tall cup of iced drink.

Betsy turned away and carefully balanced the plate and the drink. But somebody bumped her, she stumbled and fell flat on the ground.

A voice above her exclaimed, "A catch worthy of the Red Sox, but the drink fouled out!"

Betsy looked up at a gray-haired Anglo woman who was laughing down at her. Betsy didn't know what she was talking about but noticed that she had neatly caught the flying plate without spilling a bean. The drink, however, was spilled on the grass.

"Come on," the voice said, and a hand pulled her to her feet. "Let's get a refill."

Betsy picked up the empty cup and followed her back to the table where her aunt gladly provided another.

"Where to?" asked the woman.

Betsy led her through the crowd toward Grandfather. The Superintendent loomed in front of her.

"Well, Betsy, I see you have already met a daughter of Dr. Kidder," he remarked.

Betsy had heard the name, but she couldn't quite remember where.

"Yes, Betsy," said the new friend, who seemed a strange mixture of very young and very old. "This must feel like coming home to you. It does to me, too. When I was growing up, I spent many happy summers here with my family. We had a camp down there on the other side of the creek. Every day, with my sister and brothers, I came here to watch the digging my father was supervising and to see what had been found. You should have seen the mountains of pot shards my mother washed and sorted. Your ancestors certainly made and broke a lot of pottery over the years."

Betsy didn't know what to say to this, so she just continued leading the way to Grandfather. He and Mother were now sitting on folding chairs, Mother holding Baby Brother. Father jumped up and offered his chair to the newcomer, who apparently knew Grandfather already. Brother Sam was sitting on the grass nearby. Betsy felt a bit nervous about what he might say next.

And rightly so.

Sam listened to the introductions and conversation for a few minutes before joining in. "Didn't your father realize it was wicked to dig up the bones of our ancestors and take them away?" His tone was hostile. "What did he do with them anyway?"

Grandfather reached down and put his hand on Sam's shoulder to quiet him. Mother rolled her eyes. Father's face showed a mixture of irritation at Sam's rudeness and curiosity about how their guest would respond. Betsy watched her face anxiously.

But their visitor chuckled down in her throat. "Sam," she said, "those are questions people ask me all the time. The answer to the first one is, NO. My father did not feel wicked or guilty in uncovering and sending away the skeletons of your ancestors. It was part of what archaeologists did then. Human remains and the grave goods buried with them have helped scientists learn a great deal about ancient people and how they lived. It's not just Indian people they have examined, but ancestral remains from all over the world—Egypt, China, Asia, Europe, and, of course, our own ancestors. You can read about their finds in newspapers and magazines every week. Do you remember the 'Ice Man' found not long ago in a melting glacier in Switzerland? What a lot we have learned about his life and culture! Maybe you have read about how scientists are examining Einstein's brain. No disrespect intended, just the opposite."

"But why? Who cares? Isn't it a great insult for the dead?" Sam wondered.

The guest continued, "No, Sam. Once the spirit has left the body, most of us believe all that's left is a husk that can give us important glimpses of past lives. The more we know about them the more we can understand—and respect—the ancient people and their descendants today. The technology and survival skills of the ancients are truly amazing, and humbling, for all of us. We're not just limited to our own lifetimes, but part of the whole human race that precedes and follows us. We learn from those in the past; they help us live in the present and prepare for the future."

Sam interjected again, "Didn't anybody object to removal of the bones? Where were our Pecos elders? Why didn't they protest?"

"Remember, Sam. This was in the nineteen teens and twenties. In that era, Indian people everywhere were fighting for survival on many fronts. Travel between Jemez and Pecos was long and difficult, and not many people could make the trip to see what was happening. Their protests were not heard. Things are different now. Indian voices are loud and clear, and people are listening."

Betsy looked at Grandfather. He was sipping his drink and occasionally nodding his head. She knew he believed it was wrong to disturb the remains of the ancestors, the Old Ones. Their spirits were sacred. She wondered what he was thinking. He didn't say anything. Baby Brother was getting restless, and Mother was fishing around in her bag for a cracker to entertain him. Father looked as if he wanted to say something, but didn't.

"My father wasn't just a bone collector. He was trying to develop new ways of learning about ancient people. He loved Pecos for all it could teach us.

"Look at the pueblo ruins over there, do you see the long slope spreading down into the meadow? That's the midden—the dump to you. For hundreds of years, the Pecos people tossed their trash over the edge of the cliff. Broken tools, worn out sandals, animal bones, corn husks, torn baskets and mats, bits of animal hide and woven cloth . . ."

"Tin cans!"

"Beer bottles!"

"Old tires!"

"McDonald's wrappers!"

"Junk mail!"

"Baby Brother!"

"No way," cried Mother in mock horror and clutched the baby on her lap. Sam and Betsy were catching the spirit, adding their own mental trash to the debris in the midden. But a quiet gesture from Grandfather stopped them.

Their visitor was laughing. "You've got the idea! Well, over the years dirt sifted in and the trash compacted down into layers of soft earth.

"When my father started work here, he had his workers dig several trenches all the way down through the midden. The oldest things, of course, would be on the bottom with newer things above. He kept careful records of everything he found, layer by layer. The bits of broken pottery they found, more of them than you can possibly imagine, became important to help date things. You know that pottery styles and decorations change over the years, and we're talking about hundreds of years. So an object associated with a certain style of pottery shard apparently came from a particular era. It wasn't exact dating, but the best system at that time, and here it was used for the first time in the Southwest. And when metal and scraps of wool or sheep bones appeared, obviously, it was after the Spanish arrival.

"In the midden, Father found many burials, hundreds of skeletons laid to rest at different times that pot shards could help date. Do you think it's disrespectful to bury your loved ones in the dump? Some people are troubled about that and think the dead were not respected.

"But do you know what the ground is like around here? It's hard, hard, hard. The people had only digging sticks and some stone and bone tools to work with. It took a long time to dig in the hard ground. It was really a long labor of love to dig out the kivas. But bodies had to be buried quickly. They didn't want to put them in the cornfields, so what was left? The relatively soft midden and under the floors of some of the houses. So it was convenience, not disrespect, that buried so many of the ancestors there.

"Each skeleton was carefully taken from the ground and given a number. We children, of course, wished they had been given names. They were packed in boxes along with all the information gathered about where they had been found and what was buried with them. The boxes were sent to the Peabody Museum at Harvard University where the experts could examine them.

"And this is your second question, Sam. Even though only a small part of the midden and a bit of the pueblo were excavated over the years, the two thousand more-or-less skeletons from Pecos were the biggest and most important collection from any place. It covered many centuries and individuals of all ages. The experts could tell how old each person had been at death, what kinds of food they had been eating, times of famine and plenty, their diseases and injuries, wear and tear on their joints, what they had died of, if not old age. What do you suppose might have killed them?"

"European diseases!" offered Father.

"Childbirth," added Mother.

"Fighting!" shouted Sam. "Our Pecos people were warriors!"

"How about accidents?" ventured Betsy. "With all those ladders, how did they keep the little kids from falling off on their heads?"

"It was probably arthritis that made them most miserable," continued their visitor. "The constant heavy labor was tough on their joints. Some people had bent over spines that must have made every movement agony."

"How about toothaches?" Grandfather was speaking. "My grandparents used to complain about them, and since there were no dentists available, they remembered people who died from infections from broken teeth."

"Well," continued their guest, "all of those things and more. A lot of children died and not many people lived past fifty. But that wasn't much different from anywhere else in those years, from the fourteen to the eighteen hundreds. Your ancestors were tough, skillful, resourceful people, and were able to live pretty good lives here on the ridge. Their bones tell their stories and have also suggested things that can help us live healthier lives today. But perhaps, Grandfather, you could have told us that already, without the scientists' findings."

Grandfather nodded but didn't say anything.

"But Sam," she continued, "archaeologists study a lot more than bones. My father considered a lot of different things here at Pecos: houses and living patterns. The kinds of foods they raised and hunted. The tools and technology they had to work with. Their trade with distant people and how new things like those the Spaniards brought changed their lives. How they raised their families, the impact of their spiritual lives, and their relationships with other kinds of people. What they did for fun and the arts they created. So many questions were explored, and are still being investigated. Many of these findings are helpful to the current descendants who have forgotten them.

"There are some excellent Indian archaeologists now who are using their knowledge of the past to help their people in the present. I understand there are some good ones at Jemez. Perhaps you'd like to talk with some of them and learn more about what they do now and why. It's not only about bones."

Betsy was fascinated, listening with growing excitement. "Me too?" she pleaded.

Their visitor grinned at her. "Of course, Betsy. You too!"

They all sat in silence for a moment, surrounded by the hubbub of many people milling around and talking.

Then their guest reflected, "Yes, it's time for the Ancestors to come home to this place we all love. They've been away too long, some for seventy or eighty years. My father would be very pleased today. He and my mother are buried here at the Park, back somewhere beyond the creek. His spirit is surely welcoming them. I can feel his presence and almost hear him shouting 'Bully!' which he did whenever something

206   Part III: Still Here

excited or delighted him." She giggled. "You look puzzled. Nowadays, you kids would probably say 'Cool!'"

⌒

When the food was all gone and people were beginning to pack up for the long ride back to Jemez, Grandfather got up. "Betsy, Sam, let's stretch our legs a bit before getting in the car."

Limping a bit, they followed him along the path past the old mission church toward the pueblo, Grandfather pointing out various things along the way, things he insisted they needed to remember.

Betsy's favorite cousin Laura came running toward them. Her voice was full of joyous excitement.

"Grandfather! Betsy! Sam! Come and see what I have found!"

They followed her down the path to the Visitor Center and into the small museum, there. There, in a case all by itself was an ancient necklace with a large bone bead in the center.

"This is what I found down by the creek! My gift from the Ancestors! Do you remember, Grandfather? It's what I told you about, Betsy!"

Betsy looked at it with interest.

Sam just sniffed. "Exploitation!" he muttered.

But Betsy could see that he was no longer angry, just putting on an act.

Grandfather pushed him gently toward the case. "Look at it, Sam. What do you see?"

Sam's eyes gleamed and Betsy knew he was teasing Grandfather, one of his favorite activities.

"I see an ancient relic of our primitive people, studied by archaeologists, protected by the U.S. Government and put on display for the eyes of uncomprehending and ignorant visitors."

"Oh come on, Sam. Don't be such a jerk!" Laura protested.

"Look some more," insisted Grandfather. "What does it tell you? What does the label say?"

Sam squinted at the words. "That bone they think came from a mammoth! They've been extinct for thousands of years. Wow!" His tone turned to wonder.

Betsy was awed. "Our people have been here for such a long time!" she observed.

"Yes," affirmed Grandfather, gathering the three young people in a warm hug. "And we're still here!"

Glossary

AGUSTÍN GUICHE: The Pecos koshare who instigated the famous burlesque of the bishop's visit in 1760, reportedly killed by a bear.

ALFRED V. KIDDER: The archaeologist who excavated part of Pecos Pueblo.

ANGLO: Originally referring to a native English-speaking person; in New Mexico often refers to anyone of neither Hispanic nor Indian heritage.

ATLATL: A spear-thrower that could hurl a projectile with more force than an arm alone. Used for centuries before the development of bows and arrows.

BISCOCHITOS: A favorite New Mexico cookie.

BISHOP TAMARÓN: The butt of the burlesque, who apparently enjoyed the story.

BISON, GIANT: Enormous ancestors of the modem buffalo. Stone spear points of the ancient Folsom people have been found embedded among bison bones.

CAMPANA: Spanish, bell. Toca la campana—the bell is ringing.

CARAPICADA: "Pock Face" for the scars left on smallpox survivors.

CARRETAS: Two-wheeled carts pulled by oxen.

CASAS REALES: "Royal Houses," erected just outside the pueblo boundaries for official business.

CHICHARÓN: Fried pork rinds. Still popular.

CIBOLEROS: Cíbola—a name for buffalo on the great plains. Ciboleros— Hispanic settlers and Indians who hunted them.

CICUYE: Original name of what later became Pecos Pueblo. Both names mean "The Stone Place" or "City of Stone."

CONVENTO: The living/working building attached to the mission church.

CORONADO: The first of the "Shining Ones" whose expedition reached Pecos in 1540.

CUSTOS: The priest in charge of all the New Mexico missions.

DON DIEGO DE VARGAS: The Spanish governor/general who brought Spanish settlers back to New Mexico twelve years after the Pueblo Revolt, in 1698.

FATHER ANDRÉS JUÁREZ: The priest who built the big mission church at Pecos in the early 1600s.

FISCALES: Indian helpers of the mission priest.

FRANCESES: Frenchmen, filtering down across the country towards New Mexico in the 1700s.

GACHUPINES: "The men who wear spurs," an Aztec term for Spaniards.

GENÍZAROS: "Detribalized Indians," raised by Hispanics with little or no memory of their original heritage.

GRINGOS: An unflattering term for "Anglos" or outsiders.

HORNO: The adobe oven brought to New Mexico by Spanish settlers.

KIVAS: Underground ceremonial chambers where pueblo business and spiritual life are planned.

KOSHARE: The sacred clowns that have such an important role in pueblo life and rituals.

MAÑANA: Morning, tomorrow. Me gusta la mañana— I like the morning.

MANTAS: The black, one-shoulder dresses worn by pueblo women.

MAYORDOMO: Supervisor, custodian, "person in charge."

MESILLA: "Little mesa," the ridge where the pueblo and mission church were built at Pecos.

METATE / MANO: The grinding stones that pulverized seeds and corn kernels for flour and cooking.

MIDDEN: The "dump," beloved by archaeologists. At Pecos, the long, low slope below the eastern side of the Mesilla where debris from past centuries and human burials reveal much about the lives of the inhabitants.

MILITIA: Informal armies made up of government soldiers, settlers and pueblo allies for limited service or projects.

NAGPRA: Native American Graves Protection and Repatriation Act, passed in 1990, leading to the return of the Pecos ancestors in 1999.

NUESTRA SEÑORA SANTA MARÍA DE LOS ÁNGELES, DE PORCIÚNCULA: Our Lady of the Angels, Patron saint of Pecos Pueblo. Her picture hung in the mission church behind the altar and was removed to the Church of St. Anthony in Pecos Village when the pueblo was abandoned.

PADRES: "Fathers," usually used for the priests of the mission churches.

PILONCILLO: Brown sugar, molded in cones, a favorite import from Mexico.

PIÑONES: The nourishing little nuts from the piñon trees.

POPÉ: The leader of the Pueblo Revolt against the Spanish occupation and abuses in 1680, unifying many of the pueblos for the first time.

SÍPAPU: Small hole in the floor of a kiva, symbol of the traditional emergence of the ancestors into this world.

TABLITAS: Small wooden headboards decorated with symbols worn by women in many of the pueblo dances.

TARBOOSH: Sacred clowns, guardians of the feast day dances at Jemez.

TEWAS: Pueblo Indian people of the upper-middle Rio Grande valley; not to be confused with the Teyas.

TEYAS: Buffalo-hunting plains Indians, related to Apaches, who often traded at Pecos.

TORREÓN: Three-story towers constructed by soldiers at Pecos to watch for Comanche raiders.

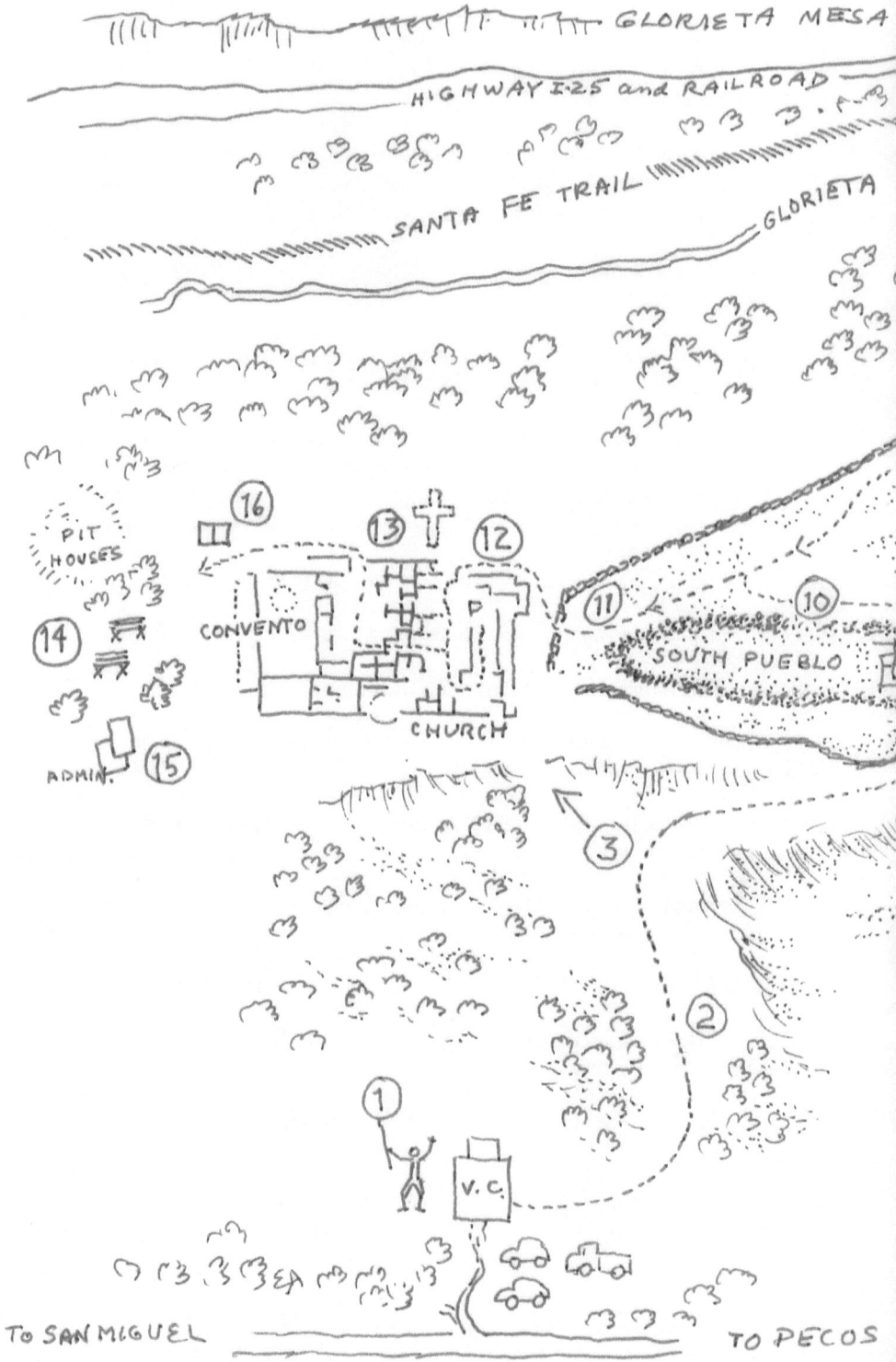

GLORIETA MESA

HIGHWAY I-25 and RAILROAD

SANTA FE TRAIL

GLORIETA

PIT HOUSES

(16)

(13)

(12)

CONVENTO

(11)

(10)

SOUTH PUEBLO

(14)

CHURCH

ADMIN.

(15)

(3)

(2)

(1)

V.C.

← TO SAN MIGUEL

TO PECOS

213

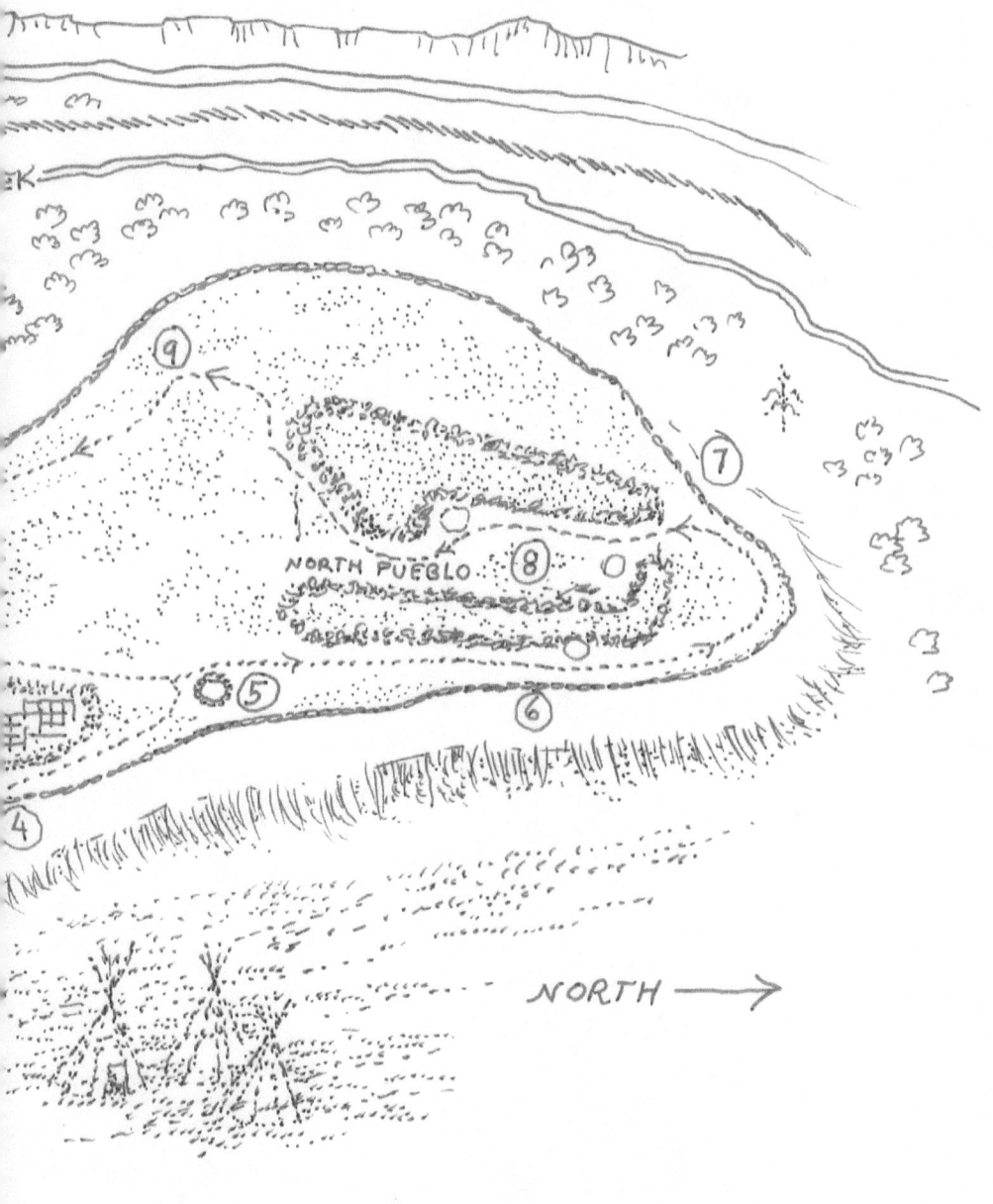

NORTH ⟶

Pecos River
1 mile
↓

LAGE ⟶

Guide for Visitors to Pecos National Historical Park

WHEN YOU WALK THE RUINS TRAIL at Pecos National Historical Park, you will see many of the areas described in these stories. Look at the map on the preceding page.

#1. THE VISITOR CENTER. A brief orientation film will help you picture the story of the ruins and the people who lived and passed through here. A small museum displays objects and pictures relating to the heritage of the area from ancient times to the present. (Don't look for the mammoth bone pendant: it's not here.) In the Pecos Room various events happen all year round. In the lobby a wide variety of books for sale can provide information and delight. And of course the rangers at the desk can give you brochures and answer many of your questions.

#2. FIRST VIEWPOINT along the Trail. Here you emerge from a wooded part of the path to a straight-ahead vista of the high mounds where the main part of the Great Pecos Pueblo once stood. Picture it at its height, 20 to 30 feet higher, 3 to 5 stories terraced back and glowing with whitewash, with people moving all around carrying out their daily tasks and ceremonies, conversations, games and social interactions. It must have been a very impressive sight. The early Spanish explorers thought so: the wayside marker quotes one of their descriptions and shows a picture of what the pueblo may have looked like.

To your right extends a broad, open field. This was the trading area, where visitors from the plains, from other pueblos, Spanish soldiers and settlers camped, and where most of the trading took place. Picture it full of tipis and people bargaining for the goods they needed or wanted. (See the picture in the round alcove in the Visitor Center.) This is where Flame almost got traded away to Bear Claws (Chapter 4).

#3. UP ON THE RIDGE in front of you the red adobe walls of the last church to occupy that site loom over you. Its ruins are nestled in the foundation of the much larger church that was destroyed during the Pueblo Revolt. The picture on the wayside sign shows what the big church may have looked like, with its six towers and its whitewashed walls.

This must have been an impressive sight, with the pueblo shining on one end of the ridge and the huge church on the other. Shut your eyes and listen: can you hear the big bronze bells echoing over the landscape— BONG, BONG, BONG—and the thumping of the drums and the sounds of the bird-bone flutes coming from the pueblo itself? Think about the choice Little Dove/Palomita (Chapter 5) had to make! What would you have done?

#4. THIS LOW WALL halfway up the slope marked the boundary of the pueblo itself. At night and certain other times all strangers were ordered outside this wall.

From here you can see the extent of the trading field today, though the visitors' need for firewood must have cleared the trees away for a long distance all around. (Chapter 4.) Picture Coronado's huge army—soldiers, animals, Indian helpers, and the "horses that ate children" camped there with everything so strange to the Pecos people.

This ridge must have been higher and steeper in the time of Small Girl (Chapter 1), and this eastern-facing cliff could have killed many of the stampeding bison.

#5. This is ONE OF THE TWO KIVAS restored by the Park Service, and yes, you can go into it. Since the spiritual life of the community, and the kivas that were so much a part of it, were the responsibility of the men, women seldom entered and therefore the stories say little about them.

This kiva now seems like a cool, dim hole in the ground. When it was "active," the walls would have been whitewashed, reflecting the light, with sacred images painted on them. A built-in *banco,* softened with skins or blankets, would have provided places to sit. Pegs in the walls would have held ceremonial gear, with handsome jars in niches for smaller sacred or ritual objects. There also would have been small looms anchored between the roof beams and hoops imbedded in the floor, where the men wove the kilts and sashes used in the dances.

The small hole in the floor is the *sípapu,* representing the "place of emergence," through which the ancestors, source of all wisdom, came into this world from their underworld home—according to pueblo creation myths. The fireplace under the hatchway often burned fragrant cedar wood, and people coming and going through the smoke would have been ritually purified. The square hole beyond the ladder is the ventilator shaft, bringing cool air in to replace the warmer air rising through the hatchway.

There were many kivas in the pueblo. In them the different clans planned and prepared for the dances and other ceremonial events for the varying seasons of the year. Here they taught the young men the heritage of the people and what they needed to know to maintain the spiritual life of the community. (See Chapter 3 about Willow's brother's apprenticeship.) And of course, the elders carried on a lot of planning and politicking about the internal and external affairs of the pueblo, as Grandfather did in most of the Great Pueblo chapters.

#6. This is where DR. KIDDER (1915-1929) dug deep trenches through the midden—the trash heap—to develop the first chronology of the artifacts found here and throughout the Southwest. Above you, the collapsed walls of the pueblo still look impressive. Below you, the broad slope of the midden extends down to the trading field all along this side of the ridge. Most of this area was never excavated. The two thousand (more or less) burials uncovered there were sent to Harvard University where they revealed to the scientists incomparable information about the life of the people throughout the centuries. In May of 1999, these ancestors were returned for reburial "somewhere" in the Park, their ancient homeland (Chapter 10).

#7. This SMALL SHELTER overlooks part of the valley of Glorieta Creek. This is where Laura (Chapter 9) slid down the slope and found the corn plants that Grandfather had planted earlier and the bone bead in the mud beside the creek. The Santa Fe Trail passed just beyond the creek (Chapter 8).

#8. Here is what remains of the PLAZA OF THE GREAT PUEBLO that figures in most of the stories in Chapters 4 to 8. Now it looks singularly unimpressive because the collapsing house blocks filled in much of the space. (See Cousin Katie's reaction in Chapter 11, do you share it?) Try to imagine the houses rising three or four stories high all around you, enclosing space for the community life of the people. Can you "hear" the kinds of sounds that might have echoed through this plaza?

Go up the steps to the high point that would have been twenty to thirty feet higher. Even now, the view sweeps out in all directions. To the north, you can see the Sangre de Cristo Mountains, often topped with shining white snow. The notch with the distant peak behind it shows where the Pecos River emerges from its canyon to flow down the eastern side of the valley just this side of the hills beyond. If the light is right, you can make out the gap in the hills to the west where the pass leads to Santa Fe and the Rio Grande area. To the west, you look down on Glorieta Creek, all along which small farm plots grew corn, beans, squash, and other crops introduced by the Spanish. Beyond the creek, the freight wagons trundled "wonderful" goods from Missouri to Santa Fe and beyond. Up the slope a little farther you can see 1-25 and the railroad that carry goods and passengers through this time-honored pass now. Behind them rise the steep cliffs of Rowe Mesa—there must have been many small tracks leading up to the top, but they are difficult to discern (Chapter 6). Follow the line of cliffs to the south, and the way to the Great Plains opens out farther down the valley. About a mile down the creek are the Forked Lightning

Ruins, where Willow's grandmother was killed by raiders. About another mile downstream, the creek joins the Pecos River. In this area, the Bison Hunters (Chapter 1) and the Basketmakers (Chapter 2) had their camps.

Beyond the Trading Field, you can glimpse the road that runs through the Park. To the left, it leads to the village of Pecos about three miles away. Some fifteen miles to the right is San Miguel del Vado. Mexican ranches and homesteads were scattered along the Pecos River between the two places (Chapter 8).

At its height, Pecos Pueblo controlled all the land you can see in every direction.

#9. This spot gives you a BROADER VIEW DOWN THE VALLEY of the creek where the ground slopes away from the Mission. At different times, you would have seen farm fields, or flocks of sheep and goats, or the pueblo horse herds, or pig sties of the Spanish soldiers stationed here to fight off the Comanches, or fruit trees, or many other indications of the changing lifeways of the people. Nearby, humps in the ground are probably remains of additional collapsed housing. Beside the trail, you can usually see bits of pottery or fragments of tools from long ago: look at them and put them back where you found them! And wonder who might have made them, when, for what purpose, and what stories they could tell if they could talk!

#10. This SOUTH PUEBLO was another huge housing block. Part of the walls are uncovered so that you can glimpse what the rooms might have looked like (this is said to be the second-floor level), but the rest of it is still covered over with earth. Some say that the more "Christianized" Indians moved into this area to be closer to the church, while the more traditional people stayed by the main plaza. Here is where Lupe lived (Chapter 6) and where the Old Hermit and his son (Chapter 8) tended their goats.

#11. The WAYSIDE PICTURE here shows what the huge church built under Father Andrés Júarez' supervision (Chapter 5) may have looked like. Notice the size of the people compared to the walls! Some 300,000 adobe bricks, each weighing between 40 and 80 pounds, were used in the construction. Imagine the labor involved in building, roofing, and whitewashing this huge structure. In the 1600s, visitors reported that this was the biggest church north of Mexico City!

Notice where the pueblo boundary wall is located, and the stone foundations of the big church just beyond the path.

#12. TWO WAYSIDE PICTURES here show what the ruins looked like in 1915 when the archaeologists began work here, and how the second church from 1716 probably appeared.

Follow the path into the church itself. You can see how much larger the original church was than its post-insurrection successor. You are (probably) standing where the high altar was located; the builders of the second church reversed ends. The beams protruding from the ruined walls are mostly original: on the underside of some of them you can still see some of the original carvings by pueblo carpenters.

The wayside picture in front of you shows what the interior of the church might have looked like, with its handsome carving and the painting of Our Lady of the Angels hanging behind the altar. This is where the rooster disrupted the mass (Chapter 7) and where the annual Pecos Feast Day (Chapter 11) is held.

Go up the altar steps and through the archway to the right and look out over the *convento* ruins before exploring the *convento* itself. Parts of the *convento* were two stories high, and surely rooms were added or removed according to need over the years. Let your imagination help you visualize what might have happened here.

#13. You pass what was an OPEN COURTYARD (see flagstones) with a drain that carried rainwater to a cistern just outside the walls, and a variety of rooms of different sizes and shapes. Most of the rooms apparently had fireplaces: the need for firewood must have been immense. The rock piles at your left supported posts that held up a brush roof to protect visitors' horses and mules from the sun or rain, Beyond, the semicircular structure was the *torreón*—the watch tower—three stories high, from which the Spanish soldiers watched for the Comanches. The large square room in the corner with a smaller square structure in the middle is believed to have been the kitchen (Chapter 5) where many people were fed. Storerooms, classrooms, workshops, meeting places all have to be imagined. What's a kiva doing in the *convento*? Apparently, the Pecos wanted to "reclaim their sacred space" after the Pueblo Revolt and used it until the return of the Spanish. When the returning missionary priests discovered it there, they filled it in with sand and built over it, and it was not rediscovered until the late 1960s. The long room with cobbled floor may have been a stable, and the large enclosure beyond may have been a sheepfold. But however it was organized, this is where the changing life of the Mission took place, and it profoundly changed the lives of the Pecos Pueblo people.

#14. On the way to the PICNIC AREA, look at the wayside sign on your right. It shows what a pit house of the 800-1000s might have looked like. A village of seven or eight of them have been found nearby, but have not been examined very closely or excavated much.

At the picnic area, the ceremonies and conversations after the reburial of the ancestors (Chapter 10) took place. Can you imagine some 1,500 people gathered there under the trees, all in their best clothes and celebrating the momentous occasion?

#15 & 16. TWO IMPORTANT PLACES. The first is the Park Administration Building where many of the professional staff work and plan and organize; the second is rest rooms—essential about this time.

So enjoy this portion of Pecos National Historical Park (there's more, much more!). Enjoy your picnic, wander the trail, look at the views, and may the spirits of the people in the stories help welcome and host your visit—Small Girl, Wonders, Willow, Flame, Little Dove/Palomita, Shell, Carapicada, Young Corn, Laura and Betsy, and their grandfathers, their mothers, their brothers, and other people portrayed.